A Badge or an Old Guitar

by

Randall Franks

**Thanks to Rachel Brown Kirkland
for her contributions!**

**Peach Picked Publishing
ISBN: 978-0-9849108-7-8**
P.O. Box 42, Tunnel Hill, Georgia 30755
*Town street insert included on cover:
Shirley Wheeler*
All other cover and interior artwork:
©2016 Randall Franks Media
Book Design: Randall Franks

Dedication:

In memory of THREE of my fathers — Floyd A. Franks, who shared with me a lifetime of story telling and left us way too soon; Grand Ole Opry Star Jesse McReynolds, who taught me to never stop dreaming; and TV legend Carroll O'Connor, my television "Pops," who inspired my interest in creating stories to entertain millions of TV viewers and readers.

Read Randall's weekly columns at
http://randallfranks.com
Randall Franks Fan Club
P.O. Box 42
Tunnel Hill, GA. 30755
Also visit him on Facebook, Twitter, and YouTube.

Randall Franks

Chapter One

Randall Franks — Chapter One

Officer Will Raines pulled his gun from its holster as five officers moved through the front yard of a dull gray mill house with covered windows and weeds as high as the porch. Sergeant James Randall stepped out from behind the lead police car, his blue eyes scanning the surroundings in the quiet McKinney, Georgia, neighborhood. He tilted back his gray Stetson hat, revealing a shock of straight, brown hair.

Quickly, he moved toward the house as Will fell in behind him. Motioning to two other officers, Randall spoke barely above a whisper.

"You two, take the back," he said. "Will, you and Roy Jr. come with me. We'll take the front."

He had been taking charge or working his way toward taking charge in such situations for the better part of twenty years, and he knew well which officers would have his back.

Will, slow-witted, heavy, and only in his twenties wouldn't have landed on the top of any job application file, but Randall, who had just turned forty, knew from experience the young cop would be there when he needed him most.

Then there was Roy Wilkes Jr. Ten years didn't make much of a difference now, but when Randall became an adopted member of the Wilkes household at age thirteen, Roy Jr. was still toddling around in training pants, and Randall was a skinny pile of knees, elbows, and acne cream. The camaraderie they had forged over the next thirty years was thicker than blood.

Outside of McKinney, everyone remembered 1963 as

9

the year the world lost one of America's greatest presidents; but for Randall, it was a blur of tragedy that he came to accept in staccato. Mountain crash. Two dead. Their names: Anthony and Frances Randall.

"Mind if we stop for pizza?" Will said as they reached the steps to the front door.

"Pizza! That's a great idea," Randall said.

The three moved toward the door with guns drawn. Randall knocked.

"McKinney Police... Pizza delivery!" he said.

Since the crash, the McKinney Police Department had been a rock of stability in Randall's life. It started when Chief Roy Wilkes, his father's best friend, provided for him as one of his own after Anthony's death. It continued as Wilkes groomed him to think like a law officer, train like a law officer, and finally, become a law officer. He knew little else. Sometimes, he was little else.

The door opened to reveal Ches, a twenty-five-year-old with short blond hair featuring a purple streak over the left ear.

"Police! Put your hands in the air!" Randall said as inside the front room two long-haired white men in their twenties — Snake and Stick — made a break for it, knocking over a table in the center of the room that held large bowls filled with pills of different colors. They didn't even take the time to push any of the piled up cash into their blue jean pockets. Instead they allowed it to scatter onto the floor as they scurried through the house like rats.

As Ches started to slam the door, Randall kicked the door, and the three policemen moved quickly into the front room of the house. Ches landed on the floor, after getting hit by the door. He cowered and reached his hands in the air because he did not wish to get shot. He covered his head and cried, "Don't shoot, don't shoot!" Roy Jr. cuffed him as Randall and Will split up almost instinctively and followed the other two. Without taking his eyes away from what was in front of him, Randall radioed to the other officers to let them know two suspects tried to escape out the back.

Snake had slithered through what once served as a dining room and knocked over anything in his path. Will moved after him cautiously, examining each opening for the strike of his prey.

Stick made his way up the stairs, ducked into a side room, and then hid behind a bedroom door. He stood poised with a large painted red clay flower pot in his hands, just waiting for the chance to crush the skull of whoever found him.

Trained for the task through years on the force, Randall instinctively fell back on the lessons he learned from the school of hard knocks: move slowly, check each room, always be on guard. Finally, he entered the last room. Stick, fearing his capture, stiffened and raised the pot.

As Snake made for the back door, it opened and the other three police officers stood ready with guns trained on him. Snake raised his hands with not even a rattle as

Will motioned them to take him away.

Will called on the radio for Randall and received no response. He moved slowly back through the house, keeping his gun at the ready. Back against the wall, he crept up the stairs and aimed ahead of him.

Lying on the floor unconscious with pieces of the flowerpot scattered about him, Randall was dazed but opened his eyes slowly. Stick, wearing a blue flannel shirt, used all his strength to try to open a window.

Meanwhile, Randall reached for his gun, then realized it was not at his side. He pulled himself up against a wardrobe, and with each passing moment he became more amused by the efforts of his newly found room-mate.

After he scanned the hall from the top of the stairs, Will saw no one. He methodically eliminated each room, scanning them for hidden danger as he heard Randall down the hall.

"Friend, I hate to tell you this, but that window won't open," Randall said, coolly. "If you jump through it, you're liable to get all cut up. Dr. Thurmond, down at the morgue, he just hates it when a body's all cut up like that."

Stick looked back at him on the floor in disbelief.

"You're crazy, man!" he exclaimed. "Jumping through that window won't kill me."

Randall smiled.

"No, no, it won't, but I'm afraid the bullets in his gun will."

He looked up toward Will who was standing in the doorway, Glock pistol pointed.

Randall Franks — Chapter One

Stick didn't miss a beat. He reached his hands toward the ceiling. Will handed off his Glock to Randall and moved in to cuff Stick.

"Where's your gun?" Will asked.

"I guess it's on the floor somewhere," Randall said. After the suspect was in cuffs, Randall handed Will's piece back to him and leaned down to scout the floor. He found his own gun beneath the spring coils of the bed.

Roy Jr. was now at the door in time to take the man downstairs.

"Need a hand, Sergeant?" Will asked, as he saw his legs sticking out from under the bed.

"No, I got it," Randall said.

Randall threw out a shoe, some socks, and a pizza box — all from under the bed.

"Are you sure you don't need a hand?" Will asked.

"No, Will, I got it," Randall said.

Will picked up a piece of the broken flowerpot and examined it.

"One thing about it, Sergeant," Will said.

"What, Will, what?" Randall said.

"No matter what they hit you with, your head always wins."

Randall came out from under the bed with streaks of red across his forehead.

"Sergeant, you're bleeding!" Will said.

Randall reached up to feel his head, and brought the red liquid where he could see it in the light coming down from the bare light bulb that hung down from the ceiling. He smelled it, then tasted it.

"Needs garlic," Randall quipped. "It's from the pizza

box."

"Well, are you OK?" Will asked.

Rising up from the floor, Randall walked towards the window.

"I'm fine. I sure could use some fresh air," Randall said.

As he opened the window, he heard a song from the neighbor's radio float in.

"Will, do you hear that?" he asked.

Randall threw his legs out the window, jumped from the second story, then eased off the porch onto the ground to find the radio. Will walked over to look out the window.

"He must have hit him harder than we thought. He's going looney!" Will said.

A neighbor woman, Doreen, watched closely out the window through a pair of binoculars. For most of Randall's forty years, love had eluded him. He had twice come close, once nearly walking down the aisle of McKinney First Baptist Church.

At one point, shortly after graduating from McKinney High School, Randall took Roy Wilkes' advice to spread his wings a bit.

"Son," he had told him, "you have the potential to reach for anything you set your mind to. At least take some of the money you earned working at the Open Kitchen Grill and go to Staten. It's only forty miles away, and you can attend Sawtooth Junior College, take some courses, and figure out what you want to do in life."

Reluctantly, Randall relinquished his jailer's badge at

the police department and turned his attention to his studies. For all of the first week, he was consumed with algebra, biology, literature, world history, and music theory. Then one day, as he paused on a veranda to eat his bologna and tomato sandwich, he looked up to see a beautiful blonde student in a little pink skirt. It was the first time in days he had looked up long enough to make eye contact with anyone. The girl walked his way.

"Hi! I'm Liz, Liz Lawson," she said, flashing a smile. "I have fashion design with Professor Keener, and I couldn't help but notice that you always sit by yourself every day. Do you mind if I join you? I usually go out for lunch, but I'm in a hurry and just grabbed a bag from the student center. Chicken nuggets and vinegar chips. You want some?"

"Reminds me of the kids' menu at Open Kitchen where I used to work," Randall said with a grin. He stood up and held out his hand. "I'm Randall, well, James Randall, but I've gone by my last name since I was thirteen. Would you like to move over to the shade?"

So began a long, hard fall into a love relationship that would forever change him. For two years, life was a succession of one-dollar movies, concert trips to Atlanta, and holding hands in the park. With every moment together, Randall became more and more certain Liz was "the one."

As their time in school came to a close, Randall's only plans were to try to return to the McKinney Police Department. Liz told him she was moving on to finish college out west and pursue her career.

"It's been fun," she said. "I will never forget all the fun

we had."

So that was that.

Randall's heart ached as he watched her little red Mustang grow smaller and smaller in the distance. He had never thought she would actually leave, nor had it occurred to him to follow her. The thing was all her fault, he decided. She had torn out his heart and stomped that sucker flat — and he didn't even see it coming.

There would be no more college for him. He would return to McKinney, back to the protection of the McKinney Police Department. There, he would build a fortress of safety within the streets he knew, among the people who knew him. He would never leave again. He would never love again.

Those were his thoughts at twenty. Then, two years later, he met Linda Lou Lorreate. Unlike Liz, Linda Lou was born and raised right there in McKinney, and her roots in the little town ran deep. Her father, Luke Lorreate, had become a well-known defense attorney. He was talented enough to make it big somewhere like Atlanta or Nashville, but his heart was in McKinney, and he determined to make his life there.

Certain his heart would be safe with her, Randall devoted his attentions to Linda Lou, and they soon became the item around town. However, love had blinded Randall to the fact Linda Lou's head had long been full of dreams of the rest of world. So when he proposed one afternoon over an ice cream soda, Linda Lou, thinking of the companionship she hoped for as she pursued her dreams, immediately screamed with delight.

"Yes! I thought you would never ask!" she exclaimed, kissing him.

They planned to wed in three weeks, and now with the future of their relationship secure about a week before the nuptials, Linda Lou began to share her dreams of leaving McKinney and becoming a part of the world that her father had rejected for small-town life.

"There's so much more to life than this," she said. "Smart business people, people who are educated and have the potential to become wealthy — people like us, Randall — they need to get out in the world and make something of themselves."

Randall put his arm around her. She had never mentioned leaving McKinney until now. Randall's insides tore at the thought, and he brushed it aside.

"We can talk about that later," he said. "Do you have your things packed for our honeymoon to Little Falls?" The night before the wedding, Linda Lou sat down with him to talk again.

"I just have to get out of this sleepy little town!" she insisted. "This might be my father's dream, but it isn't mine. Come with me, Randall. The world is open to us — New York, Chicago, Atlanta. We can make a new life together."

"I just can't see myself anywhere else, Linda Lou. I've thought about what you said all week. My home is here. My life is here. This is all I have."

"We have each other, Randall. I thought you loved me."

"I do, but I can't leave McKinney," he said. "This is

where my life is."

"Well, this isn't where my life will be. It's simple — if you love me, you will go anywhere I ask you to go to."

"Linda Lou, there is nothing I would love more than to marry you, buy a house here, have a couple of kids, go to church socials, city festivals, and make this place our home."

Linda Lou's eyes filled with tears.

"That's not for me. I guess we'd best call off the wedding," she said.

Randall swallowed a lump in his throat.

"Whatever you think is best," he said.

Whatever fortress had been knocked down during his first brush with love, Randall now built taller and stronger than ever as his second attempt fell apart.

Chief Wilkes tried to help him rise from the ashes.

"Son, I know this makes twice you feel you've been burned, but you can't let it keep you down. It's worth it to find your purpose in life, and it's worth it to reach out and let someone touch your heart again," he said.

"I've decided what I want to do, Chief," Randall replied. "Send me to the police academy. I can do more around here than keep the jail polished."

Slowly, the chief began to smile.

"Yes, I believe you can — but Randall, that's only the beginning. God has a lot in store for you, son. Seek Him first, and doors will open for you."

With the police excitement past, nine-year old Jimmy had made his way outside from the back of his house to play in the yard. He stood up, revealing a tear in the right knee of his blue jeans, and watched as Randall passed by, still humming along to the radio.

Jimmy gripped his hands together and wiped his nose on the sleeve of his faded red T-shirt and ran up onto the porch. At the top of his voice, he yelled, "Mama! Mama! Look what I caught!" His mama Doreen opened the screen door of the yellow mill house.

The year was 1990, and the house, which was a hundred years old, still didn't look a day over ninety. Doreen leaned against the doorjamb and peered out into a darkness broken only by the porch light that beamed out across the yard.

"What is it?" she asked as she bent down to his level. As he opened his hand, a dark little bug with a bit of yellow on its back flew skyward. Its tail flashed on and off.

"Well, isn't that a sight?" she said.

Randall leaned up against one of the porches and hummed along with the radio. He had grown up just a street over. As he looked around, he could almost see himself riding down the street on his green and white bicycle.

Anthony had spent his adult life working in the textile mill while Frances worked at the local Open Kitchen Grill just off the town square. While they had hoped for a big family, Frances had a tough time when her boy was born and was told she couldn't have any more children. Randall received all of what subsequent siblings would have had to parcel out among themselves. He had an idyllic childhood, playing pickup football games with friends in Hansen's field at the edge of town, riding his bike all over town, and enjoying the freedom of small-town life.

That all changed in 1963. His father was diagnosed with lung cancer and given only a few months to live. The family found hope in a possible treatment at a hospital in Nashville. Frances worked overtime to pay for the expense and drove him to the city for treatments. Young Randall stayed with the Wilkes while they made the trips. Roy and Anthony had grown up as neighbors in the mill village while their fathers worked in the mill. Anthony followed his father's footsteps to the mill while Roy started work as a police officer, but they always remained best of friends.

Late one night at the Wilkes house, the phone rang about 2 a.m.

"Hello. Yes ... Yes ... It was Anthony?" he heard Roy Wilkes say. "Frances, too? How — how are they?"

Silence.

"Oh. Oh, dear God. Dear God ..."

The news swept over Randall like a bad dream. His mother had fallen asleep at the wheel while crossing Monteagle Mountain and had driven off the road, down a steep embankment, and head-on into a tree. The crash had killed them both on impact.

With no living relatives, Randall's fate was unsure until Roy stepped forward in front of the local judge: "Your honor, This young man is one of our own. I know we have no foster families who can take him on in our county, and I can't see sending him to a facility hours away.

"He has just lost both his parents, people who were

loved and cherished in McKinney. I think it is up to us to step up and make a place for young James Randall."

"What are you suggesting, Mr. Wilkes?" Judge Phil Murray asked.

"Two other leading McKinney citizens and business people agree with me — Joe Benton and Pearl Lee. Pearl was his late mother's employer at the Open Kitchen Grill. He will live with Pearl in the house adjacent to the restaurant. Since, as you know, she lost her husband Jordan a couple years back, and we all feel it's important that there be men in his life, Joe and his wife and I and my wife agree to provide financially at a level set by the court. Joe and I will share the duties of providing positive male influences in his life.

"Pearl will have final say in all day-to-day matters, and we will be there to back her up. Randall will be welcome in our homes as well."

The judge nodded his head.

"It sounds like a prudent alternative that will take care of all that is needed," he said.

"One last thing — and this is more for young Randall to know — we are not here offering to take the place of your parents," Roy continued. "We all loved them and simply want to finish what they would have done to see you to manhood and give you opportunities, encouragement, and hope for the future. None of us will ever ask you to call us 'mom' or 'dad.'"

"Well, son, what do you think?" Judge Murray asked.

"I don't have to leave McKinney?" Randall said.

"Not if you wish to take these folks up on their offer."

Randall felt his head spinning as he heard the words,

but he didn't have to think for long.

"Yes, I want to stay…" Randall said.

"Folks our friends from the orphan services will be needing to follow up on a few things, but I don't expect any issues," the judge said. "I will have the orders drawn up, and barring anything unexpected sign them by the end of the week."

Randall crossed the street and walked close to the yellow house and up towards an open window. As he reached the window, the song came to an end and he heard the announcer's voice.

"That song's headed straight to the top — 'Is There More to Life Than This?' by J. Randall — and folks, I hear he's a real police officer," the disc jockey said.

"My song," Randall murmured to himself.

Will walked up.

"Sergeant, are you sure you're all right?" Will asked.

"I'm more than all right. I'm fantastic."

"That's great. Are you coming? Pizza's on me."

The neighbor woman, Doreen, heard the duo as they hovered near her window, and she stuck her head out to see what was amiss. Realizing it was the man she spied through her binoculars, she primped her hair and said, "Where are you all going? I can meet you there."

"We have a long night ahead at the jail, so we will have it delivered," Randall said quickly. "Maybe Will can join you another time."

Randall reached over and patted Will on the back.

"What?" Will said.

Pushing Will towards the car, Randall tipped his hat.

"Good night, ma'am."

"So are we having pizza or not? It's still on me," Will said as they climbed into the patrol car.

"No, Will. Pizza's on me. I'm singing on the radio."

"I don't think Chief Wilkes would want you to sing on the radio. It's for official business ... But you are right about one thing — pizza is on you."

Will laughed. Randall shook his head and began to sing his song, "Is There More to Life Than This?"

"Looking out the window, you see things that can turn your heart to stone.

"In the pouring rain a little girl cries for her mama, who left her all alone..."

Randall Franks

Chapter Two

25

Outside an office tower of glass and steel sat a long black limo that shimmered in the street lights. A handful of people walked casually along a Nashville street past a man in white coveralls who stood near the wall with a bucket in one hand and a rag in the other. His night task was illuminated by passing headlights. He rubbed a shine onto the letters that protruded from the front of the building — IMPERIAL. From the limo stepped Billy Joe, a twenty-six-year-old who was wearing a black hat, black jeans, and a cowboy shirt with some bling in the shape of a longhorn across its back. Billy Joe rushed towards the rotating glass door at the front of the building.

The man paused from his work. "Evening, Billy Joe." Billy Joe ignored the greeting. The man shook his head, spit on the sign, and continued his polishing.

For a long time, Billy Joe had been pretending to be someone he was not. To fans, he was the backwoods Oklahoma boy who found success honing his talents in a small town bar, working hard to save enough money to move to Nashville and finally make it big. In reality, that Oklahoma bar was only a three-week stop on his way to Music City from a small suburban town in Oregon. Had his Mustang not broken down on the road, he would never have even stopped there.

The closest he had ever been to a cow was when he once peered at one from the other side of a fence during a dairy tour in elementary school. It didn't matter. He had the best public relations gurus Imperial could buy, and they had worked successfully to manipulate the stories that came out from the lapdog news media. The fact that his real name was Howard Mindelson was, for the most part, a secret that was well-kept under his black ten-gallon hat.

Upstairs in the lavishly decorated office of the president, powerful producer Tony Grayson spoke on the phone. He saw himself as larger than life, and to command the "respect" he believed he deserved, he required everyone except his biggest star to address him as Grayson.

The forty-year-old propped his Italian loafer up on the desk and ran his free hand through his blond hair.

"Look Sims, I pay you a lot of money to make sure my artists' records get played," Grayson said loudly. "You're telling me a multi-platinum artist like Billy Joe is being bumped by a singing cop on an Indie label?"

Sammy Sims had known Grayson for years, known him when he was a college dropout managing a Southern Rock garage band in Nashville back in 1977. With his aptitude for promotion, Grayson had propelled the band's first hit to marginal success, and Sims — a song plugger himself — had taken notice, offering him a foot in the door at Imperial Records. He had sounded his own death knell. In the years that followed, Grayson climbed higher and higher up the corporate ladder, his heels leaving imprints on the backs of everyone beneath him. The man who was once a mentor now found himself the recipient of Grayson's ruthless interrogation.

Sims' voice on the other end of the line stammered apologetically.

"What do you mean there's nothing you can do?"

A pause as Grayson listened to the response.

"You better do something, or you won't be able to pay for that divorce."

Another pause.

"You're not? You will be after I speak to your wife!"

As the conversation concluded, the beautiful Elizabeth Gaines, who was thirty-two and a corporate ladder climber, appeared in red heels and a red dress, her hair styled into an upsweep.

By now, she was Grayson's biggest rival, but when she entered the country music business ten years ago, her career appeared doomed no sooner than it had started. It began with Miraculous, the now defunct record label where she interned after graduating from Belmont College, and where she landed her first job. Soon, she was working closely with Brindy Winters and Wendy Walls — the label's most promising stars — and she was certain she had a plan to jumpstart their careers.

Label president Winton Wallenstein, however, had entirely different plans for the two, and when Elizabeth tried to go around him and present her thoughts directly to Wendy and Brindy, Wallenstein had her fired. In an incident authorities were never able to fully explain, Wallenstein died shortly thereafter when his boat mysteriously exploded on the lake. As the stars' positions on the charts continued to drop, the new leader at Miraculous refused to renew their contracts, and they joined forces and turned back to Elizabeth for help. United once again, the three began knocking on doors until they found themselves in the office of Grayson's predecessor, Leamon Fellows.

A Badge or an Old Guitar

Fellows was impressed by Elizabeth, and for the next five years Brindy and Wendy sold millions of records for Imperial, thus helping Elizabeth rise up the ladder.

When Grayson was awarded the presidency, Elizabeth was close upon his heels.

She was the current vice president of Imperial Records, at least this week, as she had managed to make the move despite being Grayson's biggest rival within the company.

"Tell Bob Wilson that I got his number too and I have the same in store for him. Gotta go, Sammy. Happy plugging," Grayson said as he hung up the phone.

"Billy Joe is here, and he's hotter than a firecracker," Elizabeth said as Billy Joe burst into the office.

"Tony, what is going on? We've got three million on this release, and we're already losing ground," he said.

Elizabeth stepped over to the bar on the other side of the office and began to pour a drink for Grayson.

"I was just talking to Sammy Sims about it," Grayson said as he got up and walked toward the bar.

"What did he say?" Billy Joe asked, accepting the drink from Grayson's hand, and beginning to pace back and forth across the room while Grayson sipped his scotch.

"The attention Randall is getting is a minor setback," Grayson said.

"It better be. I spoke with Mr. Johnson in Los Angeles. It appears Mr. Enrico is not very happy. That's not good for either of us, but it's especially not good for you."

Billy Joe stomped out of the room.

Grayson, who had since perched himself on a bar stool, got up and walked over to a display where he looked at some of his collection of Civil War artifacts. He reached in and took out a knife and examined the workmanship on the handle.

"Elizabeth, let's find this Randall, find out what kind of deal he has. We'll buy his contract and sit on him. We've got to make Billy Joe number one, which means we've got to stop Randall."

Elizabeth nodded and began to head to her office. Grayson ran his finger across the blade of the knife. As he reached the tip, the blade sliced a section of his skin. His blood began to drip.

Chapter Three

In the quiet of a small town square, streetlights shone on a dozen kids who played a game of touch football. Nearby, their parents passed the evening on park benches. Across the park on the other side of the statue of Confederate soldier Robert Henry sat three police cars in front of the McKinney Police Station. The station built in the 1930s remained unchanged and apparently without a paintbrush hitting the plaster or the dark mahogany doors in decades. Inside the doors was a squad room with a large green and yellow counter across the front and dark wooden desks scattered behind it. The walls in the squad room were a color somewhere between off-white and yellow.

Officers George and Waldron were moving Ches, Snake, and Stick down the hall toward the jail cells downstairs. Randall and Will were seated at two desks filling out some paperwork. In the middle of the squad room was one lone mahogany door, and on it was painted in gold letters "Chief of Police."

The door opened with a creaking noise that reflected the horror films of old, and from his office came Chief Roy Wilkes in all of his sixty-four years. On his best day, he could only be described as gruff after getting up on the wrong side of the bed. He stood about five feet, seven inches, but still had a presence and stoutness about him that told you he could tackle someone twice his size. The years had turned his remaining hair white, but he managed to comb whatever was left in a circular fashion over his head in a way no one would notice what had let loose over time.

A Badge or an Old Guitar

Randall's thoughts drifted back over the years.

Roy, an only child, grew up in the McKinney mill village breathing in the cotton fibers that floated in the air. By the time he was grown, he knew he wanted to do something different with his life, and police work found him as a department opening arose at about the same time as did his need for a job. After fourteen years of climbing through the ranks, he was appointed chief of police at age thirty-four. The work supported him and his late wife Maria as they raised their son Roy Jr. and later helped in the final few years of Randall's youth. Seven years ago, tragedy struck the little family. It crept upon them with all the foreshadowing of every other ordinary day. Maria put on her winter coat and pulled out of the drive in the little sedan she always took to town on the same day of the week she always went grocery shopping. She drove to the same store where she had bought ground beef and canned tomatoes for the last fifteen years. Then, two hours later, as darkness began to fall, she drove down the same road that always led her home, past the same landmark majestic live oak that had stood in that same soil for the past one hundred years. Only this time, the oak was lying across the road.

Maria couldn't stop.

The day they buried her at the old church cemetery was the day each of them began desolate walks with their own grief. Roy pushed the heartache deep down inside his soul and barely mentioned her absence except for slipping quietly to her graveside each week to talk with her. Roy Jr. filled the void with vice. There were off-duty fights, nights spent in a drunken stupor, and a temper that seemed ever ready to fly off its handle. In time, with Randall and the chief's steady understanding, Roy Jr. accepted his new reality.

Loss was nothing new to Randall, but Maria's passing reignited old memories. There was the car accident that took his parents when he was thirteen, but that was only the beginning. Eight years later, his adopted mother, Pearl, was killed by a disgruntled electric company worker on a shooting spree when she happened to walk into the regional power company office at the neighboring county seat of Tindale. Then he lost Maria to a falling tree, and, later, his Aunt Louise, Joe's wife, to cancer.

"Hearts are delicate things, buddyroe," Uncle Joe once told him in the months after losing Aunt Louise. "The strong ones can endure the hard times and still come back stronger than before, but even the stoutest can handle only so much before the scars begin to take their toll. Only God can soothe that kind of hurt."

"Yes," Randall had said, "but I wish he'd do it now."

"Me, too," Joe had said. "Me, too."

As time began to heal his wounds once more, Randall hardened himself to loss. Every significant female in his life, it seemed, had entered it only to leave him. Randall came to accept that people would always come and go. As much as he wanted his life to be different, he was powerless to change it. He hadn't even had a chance to tell Pearl goodbye or let her know what she had meant to him. He had wanted to kill the man who took her, but the Tindale police had done that for him the day of the shootings. She left him the restaurant and the house where they lived, but he soon decided he'd had enough of that business. He leased the restaurant out but stayed in the house and did his best to bury the pain that her memory left behind.

Randall's thoughts jerked back to the present as the chief opened his mouth to speak.

"I was having a nice, quiet evening, and y'all had to invite guests," the chief said.

"Chief, I'm sure they'll be no trouble at all; you'll never know they are here," Randall said.

The chief walked through the room and stood between the two cluttered desks Randall and Will were working at.

"That's good, 'cause you know what tonight is," the chief said.

Without a moment's hesitation Will spoke up: "It's Thursday, Chief."

His quip drew the chief's inquiry. "And what happens on Thursday?"

Randall and Will both shrugged their shoulders.

Exasperated, shaking his head, the chief exclaimed, "Where did I find you two?"

"Well, Chief, you dated my grandmother...," Will quickly volunteered.

"No, no, Will. Why don't you go over there by the radio in case somebody needs us?" the chief said.

"But Chief, folks who need us call on the phone," Will said.

With a glare that could melt ice, the chief said, "Then go stand by the phone." He turned his attention toward Randall, hoping to find someone who would understand his effort at communication.

"Tonight is Mystery Theater on WBIE," the chief said. "They solve the case tonight — after three weeks of clues. Turn on that radio, Sergeant, and get it warmed up."

Randall moved to the corner of the room where sat an old AM radio that looked like it came with the original building. He turned the knob, bringing forth the glow of the dial and the sound of fuzz in the room.

"Somebody's hit the tuning dial. Find the station, Sergeant," the chief said.

As he began to turn the knob, he feared what might come across the airwaves and he mumbled to cover the sounds, "Chief, they ... a ... might a ... Chief."

Randall found WBIE on the dial as the announcer spoke: "You're listening to WBIE, Tindale, Georgia. It's September 3, 1990. Mystery Theater is coming up next, but first we are going to try to reach one of country's hottest new stars by phone. I'm dialing..."

The police station phone rang and Will quickly answered before the ring was complete. "McKinney Police. May I help you?"

The announcer said, "Hello, we are live on WBIE. Is J. Randall available?"

Hearing this from both sides, a puzzled look began to flit across the chief's face as the look of a kid with his hand caught in the cookie jar overtook Randall.

"Sergeant," Will said.

"Sergeant James Randall, may I help you?" Randall said.

The announcer continued: "Is this the J. Randall who

sings "Is there more to life than this? I'm Danny Day from WBIE, and we are live on the air."

A huge squeal came from the radio.

"Just a minute. Will, turn the radio down. This is he," Randall said.

The chief and Will moved closer to the radio.

The announcer asked: "Well, Sergeant Randall, how does it feel to have the fastest rising song in country music?"

Randall squirmed awkwardly in his shoes.

"I'm just happy to hear my song on the radio," he said.

The announcer's questions continued: "Sergeant Randall, do you plan to leave the police force and pursue music full time?"

As this question came across the radio, Randall felt that same stare that Will saw moments before boring into the back of his neck. He turned to find the chief looking at him, awaiting an answer.

It was a ridiculous question anyhow. Didn't the DJ know this was a work of passion? He wrote the song because he had to write it. It was about his parents, his beloved aunts. It was love and loss, passion and heartache — his own along with that of the rest of the world. It was all rolled into a few verses, and then, in those same lines, was the answer to it all. That song was there in his heart, banging around in his head at night, hammering at his brain all day, until he finally stopped one evening and wrote down all the words in one soul-quenching exorcism. But Randall couldn't share that story on the air. After all, it was Uncle Joe's story, too.

"I'll have to get back with you on that," Randall said

quickly.

"Well, Sergeant Randall," the announcer said, "I'm gonna make you and all our listeners happy with your smash hit 'Is There More to Life Than This?' followed by Mystery Theater. Goodnight, everyone."

Randall sat on the edge of the desk and hung up as his song came over the radio. The chief looked toward him as the notes came across the airwaves.

Randall was oblivious to what was going on around him as in his mind's eye he saw himself singing the song in his own music video. As the song came to an end, Will stood next to Randall trying to pull him back from the depths of his daydream.

"Sergeant? Woo-hoo, Sergeant?"

As a glimmer of recognition became apparent, Will continued: "See, I told you he wouldn't like you singing on the radio."

The chief still stood by the radio, his face blank as a newly washed chalkboard. He slowly walked over to Randall.

"Sir, I know," Randall started to say as the chief held up his hand for him to stop.

"Not bad. Not as good as Johnny Cash, but not bad. Now, after Mystery Theater, you and I are gonna have a little talk," the chief said.

"Yeah, a little talk," Will added.

"In private," the chief said, glaring at Will.

Without a moment passing, Will nervously said, "Yeah, you two will talk in private. I'll stand by the phone."

The chief barked, "Now, quiet!!! Mystery Theater is

coming on."

    Radio drama music from the 1940s began to fill the office.

Randall Franks

Chapter Four

The McKinney Police squad room was quiet. The lights were low. Randall sat at a desk, and the chief stood and waited for Randall to say something.

"OK, son. What is it you hope to do with your singing?" he asked.

"Chief, all I've ever wanted to do with my life is help folks. Working for you, I've helped a lot of people," Randall said.

The chief walked over to another desk and sat down. As he spoke, he propped his legs up on a wooden chair by the desk.

"You have, yes, you have; but are you gonna work for me or are you gonna sing?" the chief asked.

Randall got up and walked toward the reception counter. He shuffled in a small circle as he hunted for his answer.

"I'm not a singer, Chief. I'm just a police officer. That's what I'll always be. God gave me a song. I thought it might help some folks to hear it," Randall said.

"How did you get into this then?" the Chief asked. "You remember when Aunt Louise passed away last year of pancreatic cancer, Uncle Joe seemed to just ball up inside himself," Randall said. "He barely opened the music store, even stopped the music club for kids. You know Unc and Aunt taught me how to play most of the string instruments. So, I decided the best way to break him out of his despair was to engage him in music. I thought if I could get him into the studio helping me, I could bring him back."

"So, where did this song come from?"

A Badge or an Old Guitar

"It came to me in one night, but I guess I have been working on it all my life, tucking thoughts in the back of my brain through the years as things sort of got to me or struck me."

"Like what?"

"Remember about fifteen years ago when we found that little girl Josie Watson?"

The chief nodded.

"Yes. Her mother abandoned her."

"From that I wrote the line, 'In the pouring rain a little girl cries for her mama, who left her all alone,'" Randall said. "Then the Reamly brothers when I first started out."

"Hoot killed Hollow," the Chief said. "Hoot never would say why."

"That gave me 'A brother kills a brother. For what reason, we may never know.'"

"Remember that fire over on Oak Street about five years ago?" Randall continued.

"The Stephensons fought over what they had and ended up with nothing," the chief said.

From that, I wrote 'Two who loved each other, burn themselves out of house and home.'"

"So did everything in the song come from things you saw here in McKinney?" the chief asked.

"Much of it, yes. Some is simply my thoughts on things I have seen in other parts of the country from the news."

"Is there a purpose for the song?"

Randall bit his lip.

"The main purpose is to give people hope, that there

is much more to life than these terrible things. That's what the chorus is about — 'I tell you my friend there is, he gave his only son and then; A chance for us to live again; A heart that is like new, that sees the good in all we do; Yes my friend, there is so much more than this.'"

"A message that the world needs to hear, again and again. So, apparently, you cracked through Joe's shell," the chief said. "For the past few months, he has been upbeat, almost driven."

"Working with him to produce the song reignited his spark, and his dreams are once again burning bright from his window on Main Street," Randall said. "He didn't waste any time. Before I knew it, he pressed up singles and sent them out to all the major radio stations. Apparently, he made some very important friends in the music business through the years. My song getting played on the radio is the result."

"Well, apparently a number of people like it, but what about all the money?" the chief asked.

"Money?" Randall said as he walked closer to the chief.

"That song of yours is gonna make you some money, son — and the record companies are gonna offer you a lot of money to sing for them," the chief said.

Randall sat down on the edge of the desk and paused momentarily.

"I never thought about making money. They do need some equipment at the Boys Club," Randall said.

"You should put some money away for the future," the chief said.

"Chief, I always get by. Helping those kids is putting

money away for the future," he said.

The chief rose and put his hand on Randall's shoulder.

"Truer words have never been spoken," he said.

Randall Franks

Chapter Five

Randall Franks — Chapter Five

The next morning, a stretch limousine drove through town and rounded McKinney Square, drawing attention from everyone as it passed. Pulling into an empty space, the limousine parked directly in front of the McKinney Police Station. A driver got out and opened one of the back doors for his passengers. Out stepped Grayson followed by Elizabeth. They looked around with a sense of disdain for their less-than-city surroundings and then approached the police station door. The limousine driver leaned up on a sign in front of the limo. It read "Chief's Parking Only."

Inside the squad room, Will sat at the communications desk. Grayson and Elizabeth entered and walked up to the counter.

"Hello. May I help you?" Will said.

"How do you do? We are here to see J. Randall. Is he available?" Elizabeth asked.

"Well, let me see," Will said as he turned around and looked at Randall at his desk.

"Sergeant Randall, are you free?" Will asked. It was a joke between the two based on a common bit of dialogue on the popular British TV series "Are You Being Served?"

"Yes, Will. I'm free," Randall retorted, completing the inside joke.

"These folks want to see you," Will said.

Randall approached the counter, and before he even reached it, Grayson turned to Elizabeth and began speaking as if he weren't there.

"He's perfect, isn't he? Great look, very marketable. Very New Country. He'll be bigger than Reba, George…"

51

A Badge or an Old Guitar

"Excuse me," Randall said. "Who are you, and what are you talking about?"

Holding out her business card across the counter, Elizabeth said: "Mr. Randall, I'm Elizabeth Gaines, vice president of Imperial Records, and this is Tony Grayson, president of Imperial."

Randall took the card, looking closely at its Imperial Records logo.

"Imperial. That's Billy Joe's label," Will said.

"Nice to meet you both. I appreciate all the nice things you said, sir, but you could have sent a card and saved a trip," Randall said.

The chief entered through the front door.

"What idiot has my space blocked out front?" he growled. "He must be a big one to leave an expensive car like that..."

He passed the duo at the counter and rounded into the squad room.

"Chief, these folks are from Imperial Records. They've come to see the sergeant," Will said.

The chief reached up and touched the brim of his felt Stetson hat.

"Nice to see you both. Hope you enjoy your visit to our fine town. It's a beautiful day to walk through town."

"I'm afraid we won't be able to stay long, Chief," Grayson said.

"Oh?" the chief said as he leaned up against the counter.

"We've just come to persuade this talented singer to come to Imperial," Grayson said.

He turned to Randall.

"You need a name," Grayson said.

"I've got one, sir."

Grayson jumped right in like he was trying to sell something.

"No, no, a single name, like Reba, Dolly, Wynonna ... What's your first name?"

"James," Randall said.

"James ... James Randall ... Randall! That's it. You'll be Randall," Grayson declared as if he'd just discovered plutonium.

Randall moved around the counter, opened the door, and stuck out his hand.

"Mr. Grayson, Ms. Gaines, thank you both for coming. I'm quite satisfied with Uncle Joe's studio and his label," Randall said.

The duo stood there continuing to plead their case but did not move out.

"I never thought that Joe's studio would amount to much. Who needs a studio in McKinney?" Chief said.

"I don't think you understand, Randall. We're talking big time here. Songs at the top of the charts, your own CD, videos, touring," Grayson said.

Randall once again stuck out his hand to shake.

"I'm much obliged to you both coming all this way, but I'm gonna stick with Uncle Joe. He's got my song played all over," Randall said.

Reluctantly, Grayson shook hands, and he and Elizabeth took a couple of steps toward the door.

"Sergeant Randall, would you at least come up to Nashville and meet with us?" Elizabeth said.

"I'll sure stop in to say 'hi' if I'm up that way. Nice to

meet you both. Have a safe trip back.

"I've got to get back to my paperwork," Randall said.

"But Randall ..." Grayson said.

The chief smiled widely.

"Now you folks enjoy your stroll through our fair city," he said. "There's a lovely restaurant on the square."

"As Mr. Grayson said, we have to be getting back," Elizabeth said curtly. "Maybe next time."

"My, you city folks, always in a rush. I just insist that you see the sights before you leave. In fact, Will can take out the street map and point them out for you. It will give you something to look at as you walk over to get your car out of impound," the chief said.

He tipped his hat and walks towards his office.

Chapter Six

Walking along a McKinney street, Grayson and Elizabeth debated their next step. Elizabeth stepped awkwardly on a crack in the sidewalk and broke her heel.

"There's got to be a way to convince him," Grayson said.

"He's one of those white hat types — loyalty, truth, God, and country," Elizabeth said as she reached down and pulled off her shoe.

They walked in front of a storefront and noticed a large sign across the building that read: "JOE BENTON'S MUSIC and RECORD SHOP." A small orange sign in the window announced: "Cut your own song! Just $400." They entered the front door of the shop.

The building was lined with aisles of shelves and display cases full of records, some new releases on CDs, videotapes, and music books. Joe, who at fifty was slightly overweight, stood near a bin straightening records. Another orange sign on a closed door read: "Studio." As an amateur musician, Randall had cut his teeth in these rooms and hallways. It was where Joe and Louise had taken Randall under their wings. It didn't matter that they were only in their twenties when they took on the mentorship. They had already begun a local children's music club to teach the basics of piano, guitar, and fiddle. Randall fit right in. Louise, who was a Samely when she dated Joe in high school, had played piano at McKinney First Baptist from her youth, and she sang like a bird.

"Hello. May I help you?" Joe said as he walked toward Grayson and Elizabeth.

"Are you Mr. Benton?" Grayson asked.

"Yes."

"I just want to shake the hand of the man who produced "Is There More to Life Than This?" Grayson said, extending his hand.

"Well, of course; and who might you be?" Joe said as he shook his hand.

Elizabeth jumped in, as she tried to soothe Grayson's ego. She planted her good shoe squarely on the ground and toed the floor carefully with her other foot.

"This is Tony Grayson, president of Imperial, and I'm Elizabeth Gaines," Elizabeth said.

"I carry your new Billy Joe CD," Joe said as he pointed to a display case full of Billy Joe products, next to a stack of J. Randall 45 records.

"It's moving a little slow," Joe said as he returned to his work straightening products.

"Looks like things are slow on Randall too," Grayson said, picking up one of his singles.

Elizabeth noticed a stack of J. Randall eight-inch by ten-inch photos on the counter next to the singles, and she picked up a couple. A four-inch by four-inch sign with the words "photo $1" inscribed in pencil hung above the photos.

"I just filled that up for the fifth time today," Joe said.

"Joe ... May I call you Joe?" Grayson began. Without waiting for an answer, he continued.

"Joe, Imperial wants your nephew Randall, but he wants to stay with you. Can we persuade you to sell him to us?"

"Sell him? He's not a turnip," Joe returned. "Randall is not my nephew. I helped raise him when his parents were killed. He just calls me 'uncle.'"

"Oh, I see. We just want his contract, the masters, the product. You could upgrade your studio — state of the art."

"Well, I've already sold several thousand 45 singles, and Walmart's distributor called just today," Joe said as he walked behind his counter near the old-fashioned punch button cash register.

"Mr. Benton, we can help you with your distribution," Elizabeth said, clutching the counter for balance.

"What about it Joe? I can have a check here by five o'clock," Grayson continued.

"Well, all the things you've mentioned sound great. You see, Sergeant Randall and I deal on a handshake. I have nothing to sell you except 45 singles," Joe said.

"You mean Sergeant Randall owns his master?" Elizabeth said as she looked at Grayson.

"Lock, stock, and barrel," Joe said, unruffled.

"Well, thank you, Joe," Grayson said. They moved toward the exit, but Grayson stopped, then turned around.

"Joe, I really think Imperial can make Randall a huge star. I know he values your relationship. You know what we can do for him. Will you talk with him?

"Well ..." Joe hesitated.

"I can make it worth your while," Grayson said. Joe turned red.

"Mr. Grayson, just because you buy your way around Nashville doesn't mean everyone is for sale. Good day," Joe said.

Grayson made a hasty departure. Elizabeth lingered

to make a final pitch.

"Mr. Benton, you know we can help him. Please talk to him," Elizabeth said. "Do you mind if I have these photos of J. Randall? Could I pay you?"

He waved her off from pulling out money, so she left a business card and walked out with the dignity of a woman who wasn't limping along on a broken heel. Joe stood at the counter and stared at the card.

Chapter Seven

Randall Franks — Chapter Seven

Grayson and Elizabeth struggled a bit in the heat to complete their walk to the McKinney Impound Yard. They spotted their limo, a police car, and a tow truck, and they entered the yard where they walked to a patch of gravel area shaded by a porch. Around a table sat Raymond Wilburn, an African-American in his thirties who stood about five feet, six inches, and ran the impound yard. Raymond got his job with the city of McKinney when he graduated high school. He operated the impound yard with a razor-like precision. In his heart, he was always filled with a glee tinted with a bit of mischief.

He sat and played cards with the young Latino limo driver Jason Reyes, who did not see his employers as they arrived. Officer Roy Jr. watched the duo play and noticed the arrival of the two music executives as they dragged in from their excursion.

Grayson was not too happy about the activity Jason was enjoying.

"What are you doing? Why haven't you paid the fee and come to get us?" he demanded sharply.

Jason stood and quickly pulled his black driver's cap back onto his head.

"Sir, Mr. Grayson, they wouldn't let me."

"What?"

Not missing a beat, Raymond began to beat out a rhythm on the table using his index fingers as drum sticks singing in time with his motion.

"If you want to pay a fine, you gotta do it yourself.

"A fifty-dollar bill, just a small amount of your wealth.

"Your limo awaits, and away you can go.

A Badge or an Old Guitar

"We hope your walk was nice and you learned a thing or two.

"Remember when you park, check the signs in your view!"

Raymond stood, stuck out his hand, and walked around Grayson scatting with the rhythm of his song. Grayson took out a roll of money. Quickly, he peeled off a fifty and motioned to Jason, who opened their door. Elizabeth hobbled to her ride and slid across the seat, relieved at no longer having to trek around in uneven footwear.

Grayson quickly slid in after her and glanced up to witness Raymond waving toward him while he hummed his tune. As the limo pulled from the dusty gravel lot, Raymond returned to the table and began dealing in Officer Roy.

Chapter Eight

Randall Franks — Chapter Eight

Will sat at the communications desk in the McKinney Police Squad Room clipping his toenails with a pair of industrial sized scissors. His shoes were perched on the desk. Randall was at his own desk completing paperwork when the phone rang. He looked up to see how Will would handle the situation. Will scrambled to knock off the phone receiver with his elbow without losing his place on his nail with the scissors. He held his ear down to the phone, which was now lying on the desk next to his shoe.

"McKinney Police. Yes ma'am ... What's your address? ... We'll be right there ... Don't worry!"

Will dropped the scissors and reached for his sock.

Randall was already prepared to leave.

"Where are we headed?" he asked.

"1116 North Elm. Betty James' place. Someone is firing shots behind her home," Will said.

"Let's go," Randall said as he headed toward the front door and grabbed his hat. Will still had one shoe in his hand. He hopped his way behind Randall as he struggled to put it on.

In a vacant lot at the edge of town were two boys, Les Evert and Billy Raymond, both age thirteen. Les and Billy were good boys but they always seemed to get themselves into things that helped their seats remain hard to sit on for long stretches. Les wore a pair of overalls with no shirt and was the lesser of the two by three inches since Billy had caught a growth spurt. Billy's five-foot, three-inch frame was covered in a red plaid short-sleeved shirt and jeans sporting a hole in the left knee. The boys were shooting at cans with a pistol.

"It's my turn! You said you would let me shoot!" Les said.

"I will, I will," Billy said.

Billy shot a couple more rounds.

A police car moved quickly through the streets of McKinney. Will was driving, and Randall was in the passenger seat with the window down. In the distance, they heard the gun fire another shot.

"You better cut the siren so they don't run. Come in on Oak by that vacant lot. I bet that's where they are," Randall said as he picked up the radio mike.

"Jake, you go to Miss James' door. Will and I will cover the back," he said to another officer who responded in a different car from the other side of town.

Will and Randall heard another shot. They stopped the car, got out, and began cautiously moving around the building with their guns drawn. As they got to the back of the building in the neighboring lot, they saw two boys on the ground. Billy was lying on top of Les, shaking him. The officers approach with guns still drawn, unaware of where the shots came from. They rushed to check the boys. Billy was upset.

"Les! Get up Les!" Billy said.

"Billy, what happened?" Randall asked as the two officers continued to watch for a shooter.

"Les is hit," Billy said.

Randall checked Les for a pulse and his breathing as Will continued scanning the surrounding area.

"Les, can you hear me?" Randall asked.

Les began to come around.

"Billy, is it my turn yet?" he asked.

Billy breathed a sigh of relief. Nearly falling to the ground, he lowered himself to sitting and began to shake.

"Les, you're OK. I thought you were shot," Billy said.

"Who was shooting at you boys?" Will said.

"I don't think anyone was shooting at them. Right, Billy?" Randall said.

Billy quietly pulled a gun from his pocket. He handed it to Randall.

"Where did you get the gun, Billy?" Randall asked.

Les sat up.

"It's his dad's," he said.

"Boys, you're both in a lot of trouble," Will said as he snapped the gun back into his holster.

"Have they broken any laws?" Randall asked as he stood Les up to his feet and brushed him off.

"Discharging a firearm in the city limits. Carrying a concealed weapon without a permit. Disturbing the peace," Will said.

By now, Billy was calm. He stood up and walked over to the cans they were shooting at, picking one up.

"These were what we were shooting at," Billy admitted.

"You realize bullets travel a long distance. You could have hurt somebody in those houses over there. What if Les had really been shot?" Randall chastised them.

"Yes, sir. I mean, no, sir. I mean, well … " Billy trailed off, at a loss for words.

Randall motioned for him to come over by Les.

"Boys, first thing we're gonna do is you two apologize to Ms. James for scaring her. Then we'll take a ride down and see the chief," Randall said.

A Badge or an Old Guitar

"The chief? He'll tell our parents!" Les said, furrowing his brow.

"Yes, that would be the next step," Randall replied.

"This is all your fault," Les said to Billy.

"Yep," Billy agreed.

Randall began to walk towards Ms. James' house while the boys reluctantly stood there as Les looked angrily at Billy.

"Let's go, boys," Will said.

Randall Franks

Chapter Nine

Will and Randall pulled around the town center in the police car with Billy and Les in the back seat.

Traffic in McKinney had ground to a halt as car after truck after car after truck jammed the town's live oak- and magnolia-lined streets. Every parking space was filled, and cars were backed up around the square in both directions, nearly obscuring the marble statue of Confederate Captain Louis T. McKinney, the son of the town's founder, who was killed at Missionary Ridge. Horns were honking. Several people had put their cars and trucks in park, and they had stepped out to lean against the sides of their vehicles. Many were simply using the time to catch up with one another.

"Must be an accident," Will said.

Lottie Jolly, 55, ran up to the passenger window of the car, motioning to roll it down. She was more than slightly overweight, and as she motioned, the flab underneath her arm jiggled back and forth. She wore a yellow daisy floral print polyester dress. It screamed 1970s. Lottie ran the local beauty salon and had more news in her head than the McKinney Messenger had in its one hundred fifty years of archives. She didn't hesitate sharing it either, and it didn't even cost twenty-five cents.

"Sergeant Randall! Come quick! You've got to do something!" Lottie said.

Lottie ran up ahead without filling in any of the questions that filled the officers' heads.

"Get the boys to the station. I'll see what is going on," Randall said.

He climbed out of the cruiser and headed up the street. Lottie stood there, appearing very upset.

"Now, Lottie, calm down. What is it?" Randall asked.

"Can't you see?" Lottie said.

Randall looked across the square to the front of Joe Benton's record shop. Cars and trucks were parked everywhere. Milling about were fifteen musicians with guitars, all wandering around singing. Another ten to fifteen singers were lined up in front of Joe's.

"Now, Sergeant, I'm all for music. But nobody can get in my shop, and Mrs. Peeler has a 2:30. You know how Mrs. Peeler is if she doesn't have her makeover," Lottie said.

"I know. She's a sight."

Lottie looked at him quizzically, wondering if he meant what he said.

"I mean, this is a sight. I'll see what I can do," Randall said as he made his way across the square.

"You do that, Sergeant," Lottie said, raising her voice.

"Yes, ma'am."

Randall walked away.

Lottie, with a different tone, tried to catch his attention again.

"Sergeant!"

Randall turned.

"When you finish, come by — I'll give you a manicure. A singer like you should have a manicure."

"Thanks so much, but I feel just fine."

"No, no — a manicure," Lottie repeated, attempting to explain with her hands.

"Talk to you later, Miss Lottie!"

Randall turned on his heel. He walked by a long-haired singer pounding out a rock song while leaning against a magnolia on the square. He passed a boy with a banjo in his lap perched upon a park bench like a peacock with his feet on the seat singing a mountain song. He passed two girls trying to find harmony parts on a classic country song. He finally reached the store and excused himself to make his way inside.

He found musicians everywhere and the door to the studio open. A western swing melody emanated from the studio control room and flooded the store.

Randall found Joe there sitting at his console, and through the window a singer and a couple of musicians were visible. The song came to an end.

"That was great, Tracy, but let's try once more," Joe said.

"Excuse me, Uncle Joe," Randall said.

Joe hit the talk back button.

"Take five, boys," he said. "Then go over that chorus again, and then we'll try one more."

"Hey, buddyroe, have'n a good day? I'm just cutting a few tracks," Joe said.

"I know, Uncle Joe, sounds good. Where's he from?" Randall asked as he walked over to the glass.

"Oklahoma," Joe said.

"That's a long way to come to record."

"He heard your song was recorded here. So, he thought he might have a shot like you."

"Hmmm. What about the rest of them?"

"Rest of them? Oh, you mean the Cajun boy in the store. I'll get to him soon. We've got one more and we'll have this song down."

Randall walked back toward the door.

A Badge or an Old Guitar

"Hey Unc, have you been outside since lunch?"

"I didn't even stop for lunch. There were five singers here this morning when I got here. That Cajun boy is the last one."

"I think you should step outside," Randall said.

Randall and Joe walked through the store, and then to the front door and outside to see a square filled with pickers and singers. Joe reached up, pulled off his baseball cap, and began scratching his head as he looked in every direction.

"Good golly, Miss Molly. Where did they all come from?" Joe exclaimed.

"Looking at the license plates, from all over the country. Unc, we've got to get the roads cleared up here. Ms. Jolly's worried about her customers getting in," Randall said.

"Today's Wednesday, isn't it? Mrs. Peeler is in today. Let's get the place cleaned up. Can you get their attention?" Joe said.

"You still got that bullhorn you use at the town picnic?" Randall asked.

"Yeah, I'll get it," Joe said as he rushed back into the store and began searching under his front counter, tossing things in every direction until the bullhorn was uncovered. He ran back out front and handed it off.

"Here you go," Joe said.

"Hey, everyone. Can I have your attention? Can I have your attention, please?" Randall said.

He continued after they settled down.

"I am Sergeant James Randall. This is Joe Benton. Mr. Benton will speak to you in a moment, but first, I must ask all of you to help us with a few things. First, we cannot block traffic. You can only park in designated spaces. Please do not block other business fronts. You can wait in the square until Mr. Benton gets to you. Thank you. Here, Joe."

Randall handed the horn to Joe, who jumped in, even though he was not sure what to say.

"Hello, everyone. I look forward to meeting each of you. But, I can only handle so many of you today. So, we will start a list. Each of you will get your appointment in that order."

Joe turned away from the horn and asked Randall, "Can anybody help me?"

"I've got to get to the station, but here comes Mrs. Peeler," Randall said as he made a speedy exit before she got through the crowd. Joe quickly ducked back into the store as Lottie pressed her way through the crowd from her salon front door.

Mrs. Peeler was wearing a huge red hat on her head, sunglasses only equaled in size by the sun. Her bright white dress shimmered like a sheet of diamonds. The crowd parted for her as God parted the Red Sea, and she moved unobstructed towards the chair in Lottie's salon for her 2:30 appointment.

The world could stop spinning, but at the appointed time she would be sitting in Lottie's chair for her weekly hair set, or the entire town would cease to be.

Randall Franks

Chapter Ten

Randall stepped into the McKinney Squad Room to find Billy and Les sitting side by side in the center of the room. The chief paced behind their chairs. Randall stepped in and leaned back on the counter.

"When will our parents be here?" Les asked.

The chief glared deep into his face.

"Did anyone tell you to speak?"

"No."

"No, what?"

"No, sir."

The chief turned back to his officers.

"When will their parents be here?"

"Any minute, sir," Will said.

George Evert, Les's father, a brawny man in his late thirties, entered the room wearing a pair of brown slacks and a white shirt with the sleeves rolled up to just below the elbows. He pulled off his hat, revealing a receding hairline. Placing the hat on the counter, he moved toward Les, positioning himself in front of him.

"Les, are you OK?"

"Yes, sir."

"That's great. Your mother and I were really worried about you. We're both gonna kill you when we get home."

George turned to the chief.

"Can I take Les home?"

The chief turned toward his officers.

"Let's see … Are there any charges against Les?"

"No charges, but he agreed to help out Ms. James with lawn work for the next month," Randall said as he moved toward his desk and took a seat.

A Badge or an Old Guitar

"OK, George. Take him home. Les — I don't want to see you in here again in trouble," the chief said.

"Yes, Chief," Les answered.

"He'll be lucky to be seen by his fourteenth birthday …" George declared. "Thank you, Randall."

Father and son left as George gave Les a gentle shove through the front door.

"OK, Mr. Billy Raymond, it's all your show now," the chief said.

Just then Ray Raymond pushed open the door to the room, his face twisted in anger. Even now at forty years old, he was known around town as a classic troublemaker — and his outward appearance made no arguments for a better reputation. Unshaven, and wearing a dirty T-shirt and faded jeans with holes in every place they shouldn't be, Ray was angry, unkempt, and seemed ready to explode at any minute. Randall and Will rose quickly to their feet.

"What right do you have holding my son here?" Ray demanded.

"Excuse me?" the chief returned.

"Why have you got my son here?"

"'Cause Billy decided he wanted to borrow your gun and do a little can hunting in the neighborhood," Chief said.

Ray stormed behind the counter toward his son.

"Is that true, Billy?"

Too afraid to answer, Billy just sat there quietly, his eyes downcast. He began to shake his right leg up and down against the chair.

"Is that true, Billy?" Ray repeated.

This time, Billy managed a barely audible reply.

" … Yes, sir … "

Ray took a step back, put a hand on his hip, and seemed to be calming down.

"What am I gonna do with you?" he said.

Randall interjected.

"When we arrived, Billy and Les had been fighting over the gun. It had fired, and we thought Les was shot."

"He wasn't, was he?" Ray asked.

"No, thank God."

Ray walked back around in front of Billy.

"You realize you could have killed Les?"

Billy continued his silence as fear took its grip on his faculties. Ray, once again reaching a fever pitch, did not let up.

"Do you?! I don't know what I'm going to do with you!"

Ray turned away and fumed at the wall.

"Now, Ray, we've all shot our share of cans," Chief said. "And at his age, I, myself, got into my fair share of mischief."

"I did too, Ray," Randall added. "The boys are gonna do some public service helping Ms. James …"

Before Randall could continue, Ray turned back to Billy and exploded.

"You are such a screw up! Do you hear me, screw up!? I'm going to make you wish you were never born, you idiot! Take my gun and nearly kill someone!"

"Now, Ray, settle down," Chief said. His voice was calm but authoritative.

Randall moved to get in between Ray and Billy.

83

"Mr. Raymond, there is no need for all this," Randall said.

Ray turned his anger toward Randall.

"You keep out of this. This is between me and my son!"

Ray pushed by Randall toward Billy who had begun to cry.

"When I get you home ..." Ray muttered angrily.

"Please, Mr. Raymond!" Randall said, trying to separate Ray from Billy.

Ray pulled loose, falling to the floor as he did so and sending Randall crashing down on top of him. The chief helped them both up.

"Are you both OK?" Chief asked.

"My arm — you broke my arm! Chief, I want this man arrested for assault and battery!"

"What?" Randall exclaimed.

"Assault and battery, Chief."

Ray turned to Randall.

"Did I hit you? Did I hit my son? Why did you knock me down?"

"I didn't mean to hurt you."

"You broke my arm. I want him arrested, Chief."

"Settle down. I'm sure we can work something out," Chief replied. "First, Will, take Mr. Raymond and Billy over to Dr. Lawson's. Billy, you don't forget your public service."

"No sir, I won't. Thank you, Sergeant Randall," Billy said.

"Ray, we'll speak a little later," Chief said.

Standing like a deer in the headlights, Randall

watched them leave the room.

"I'm not kidding, Chief. Arrest him!" Ray repeated.

"Chief, I was defending the boy," Randall said.

The chief paused as he waited for the others to leave before turning to Randall.

"I know, I know, and I think I can reason with Mr. Raymond. I'm sure he wouldn't want us to press the charges against Billy. But you came between a man and his son; you hurt his pride in front of his boy. He has to do something to get it back," he said.

"But Chief, I didn't mean to hurt him. It was an accident."

"I know. For now though, I'm gonna have to suspend you 'til I get everything straightened out."

"Chief, no!"

"Just 'til Ray cools down and I talk to him."

"Fine. Am I under arrest?"

"Son, of course not. Just take a few days off."

"OK, Chief."

Randall turned to leave.

"Son, I'll need your gun — and badge."

Slowly, Randall removed first his weapon, then his badge. He placed them together on the counter.

Chapter Eleven

Grayson's limo sailed down a highway as the sun glistened off its darkened windows. Grayson and Elizabeth sat in the back seat as a cellphone rang. Grayson picked it up.

"Hello, yes, Mr. Enrico ... Yes sir. How are you? ... I'm on top of it ... Billy Joe and I won't let you down, sir." Enrico, an Italian American investment banker in his fifties, held his phone out a little from his face as he spoke into it. Whether he really was a mobster or not, his appearance certainly gave onlookers occasion to believe so, and his position as Imperial's chief financial backer protected him from questions that would have plagued a lesser-monied man.

Standing inside a Mediterranean style mansion, Enrico stepped to a window and looked out at his pool. Three beautiful women in bathing suits — one in blue, one in red, and one in white — dutifully flashed back smiles as they noticed his gaze. He brushed a piece of lint off his custom-tailored Italian suit and again turned his attention to the conversation.

Although his voice was friendly, Enrico replied in a way that reflected a more sinister objective.

"Tony, my friend, we are very unhappy in Los Angeles. If you don't deliver with this Billy Joe project, a change is inevitable — a very permanent change."

Enrico slipped the phone's receiver into its carrying case. Picking up his glass, he tipped it toward his mouth and turned his attention to the women now doing flips on the diving board outside his window.

The hum of the highway filled the silence as Grayson

reflected on Enrico's warning.

"Permanent," he muttered under his breath.

"What's that sir?" Elizabeth asked.

"Nothing. I'm putting this Randall situation in your hands. Take care of it."

"What can I do that we haven't already done?"

"Elizabeth, if you don't want to lose this cushy job, you will do whatever it takes. We've got to put Billy Joe on top and get Randall out of the way — whatever it takes."

Elizabeth nodded.

"What if I put out the word in all the fan and industry news publications and get our guy at the Tennessean to run that we had a meeting with him?" she suggested. "It can run with one of these promo photos, giving the impression that Imperial and he are in talks. That will keep everyone else away from him for a while and give us time to start working on radio to not focus as much on this song because we should have another in a few weeks. That should let Billy Joe's song get a leg up."

Grayson pressed his fingertips together and considered. Then his eyes met Elizabeth's with a look of determination.

"Have his picture on the front page on everything we can get it on this week," Grayson commanded. "Get the rest rolling. This better work — or I would suggest you update your resume."

Chapter Twelve

Later that night the light shone through the window from Joe Benton's Record Shop. Joe walked down the street. The square was quiet except for music that emanated from a couple of tents where artists were quietly playing and singing. Joe was surprised to find his light on and entered the business cautiously. He found Randall sitting alone and playing a mandolin.

"I thought someone was in here. What's wrong? You seem a little down, buddyroe," Joe said.

Randall got up and placed the mandolin back in its case.

"I don't understand Unc. How can helping someone throw my life into such a mess?" Randall said.

Joe began moving around the studio as he straightened up the room.

"You know, I heard something on that subject. I think I have it over here," Joe said.

He went over to the DAT player, slipped in a tape, tapped the forward button, and then hit the play button.

Randall's ears pricked up as he listened to the words from his own song.

" … Children who pick up a gun to get even with everyone, Who filled their little lives with hurt …"

Joe stopped the tape.

"Sound familiar? Brother, I think it's time we go to Nashville and talk to those record folks. This may be God's way of nudging you along," Joe said with a nod.

"All I ever wanted to do was help people. A police officer helps people."

"He'll open the doors he wants us to go in and close the ones we shouldn't. Singers help people too."

"Maybe so. Hey, what you gonna do about all those singers?"

Joe smiled and began turning on all the studio's lights.

"Well, let's wake a few up," he said. "As soon as we finish, we can go."

Chapter Thirteen

The sun rose over the river behind Nashville's Printer Alley. A beat-up light green Ford pickup turned onto Broadway Street. Joe smiled as he drove down the nearly empty street, and he popped Randall on the arm with his right hand, waking him up. Randall tipped back his hat, stretched, and rubbed the sleep from his eyes.

"Look, there's the ET Record Shop. That's where they have the Midnight Jamboree," Joe said as he pointed up the street.

"I know, and the Ryman is right up there. My parents saw Bill Monroe there," Randall said.

"Have you ever been up here before?" Joe asked as they stopped for a traffic light by Tootsie's Lounge.

Randall peered through the truck window into the windows of the bar. A man in torn clothes slept as he leaned up against the side of the building.

"Just as a boy. My parents and I went to the Opry. I saw Roy Acuff, Ernest Tubb, and Kitty Wells," Randall said.

Joe reached over and tuned the radio to WSM 650 AM.

"Rise and shine, morning glories!" beamed the announcer.

As the light turned green, Joe hit the gas and the truck headed straight on up Broadway.

"Well, I don't know about, you but I am hungry. How about some breakfast? I know a little place just up here off Demonbreun," Joe said. "Then we'll head up to Music Row. I want to introduce you to a friend at Superior."

"What are we having for breakfast?" Randall asked.

"No thoughts about Superior?"

"That's a big company."

"I called ahead and made an appointment. That's how everything is run up here now. When I was younger, you could see anybody. Now you can't even get in the parking lot without an appointment."

"What's the friend's name?"

"At present, the name is pancakes, sausage, eggs over easy, some orange juice, and a piece of country ham with some red eye gravy," Joe said. "But when we get to the building it will be Clayton Willows."

"Why I have heard of all of those," Randall said. "By the way, that sounds like enough for me. What are you going to eat?"

"Funny," Joe said as he pulled into a little diner. "Clayton and I go way back. He lived over to Tindale and we played in the same band in high school, and he really likes your song."

Randall Franks

Chapter Fourteen

Behind a desk in a high-rise office decorated sleekly in mahogany art deco with chrome accents sat Clayton Willows.

Clayton, an athletic man in his late forties, was a musician's musician who came to Nashville right out of high school. He played everything and came up through the ranks. His best gigs were played on the road with a dozen Hall of Famers and Opry stars. On the side, he became a studio musician, then a session leader, and soon a producer. He landed some major awards and started his own label. When that outfit began rivaling those of the big boys, Superior bought him out and quickly put him in a top position. He had worked his way up to president.

As a secretary opened the door to his office for Joe and Randall, Clayton rose to meet them.

"Come in, Joe! You've put on a pound or two," he said, chuckling.

Joe beamed good-naturedly. "Well, I see you've still got some hair!"

Joe turned to Randall. "He always worried about losing it. His dad and granddad were both bald."

Clayton's bright eyes quickly turned toward the reason for their visit as he took his hand from Joe's back and reached out towards Randall.

"This must be that new discovery of yours," he remarked to Joe. "J. Randall, I've heard a lot about you."

"Mr. Willows," Randall said.

"Call me Clayton, please. Sit, gentlemen. Something to drink? How about some iced tea?" Clayton tapped his intercom.

A Badge or an Old Guitar

"This boy's tall," Clayton said. "What are you — six-foot-two?"

"Six-one," Randall said.

"Forty-two long, right?" Clayton said.

"Yeah."

"Clayton grew up working in his family suit-making business. It's now the nationwide chain More Suits for Less," Joe said. "He could always guess people's sizes."

Clayton tapped the intercom again.

"Sarah, three iced teas, please."

Clayton paced around his desk and perched himself on its corner.

"Son, you have really stirred up things in Nashville."

"How's that, Mr. Willows?" Randall asked.

"It's been almost two decades since an independent bulleted to the top of the charts. You've got every label head shaking in his boots, Joe," Clayton said.

He picked up the latest copy of Billboard and waved it in the air.

"Including you?" Joe asked.

"No ..."

He slapped the Billboard onto his desk.

" ... Because I know I'm going to sign Randall to Superior."

"I'm happy with Joe," Randall said.

"You don't have to leave Joe. He can still be your producer. His label name can appear on the product with ours and share in the profits."

"Well, what do you think, buddyroe?"

"I don't know," Randall said.

"It sounds good, Clayton, but Randall's gonna need

some money to get on the road, bus, band equipment," Joe said.

"We've got a budget for all of that. I want Randall to be our Billy Joe," Clayton said.

Joe stood and held out his hand.

"Clayton, why don't you put everything on paper? We'll meet again tomorrow. Look it all over."

Randall came to his feet and reluctantly shook his head.

"I don't know, we're moving pretty fast. I'm not sure if I want to go on the road."

Joe placed a hand on Randall's shoulder.

"The decision hasn't got to be made now. We're just gonna look at Clayton's offer," Joe said.

"That's right, Randall. This is just the first step," Clayton said. He grinned like a car dealer nearing a sale.

"Well, we've got some sights to see, Clayton," Joe said.

Randall and Clayton shook hands, and Randall turned to walk out the door with Joe.

"I told Ms. Gaines we'd stop by and say 'Hi.'" Randall said. "We should do that before we stop to see the sights."

Clayton overheard them as he neared his desk.

"Elizabeth Gaines at Imperial?" Clayton asked, as he drew Randall and Joe back inside the door.

"Yes, she came down to the station with Mr. Grayson," Randall said.

Clayton's smile faded, and his brow began to furrow.

"Did they offer some money?" Clayton asked.

Joe spoke up quickly, as he sensed the concern in his friend's voice.

"They really want him. They came by and offered me

a check for his masters," Joe said.

Clayton walked back around the desk and closer to the door.

"Don't trust those two. They've got one agenda, and his name is Billy Joe," Clayton said.

Randall shifted on his feet. He didn't want anyone to think he was playing games.

"We're just gonna be neighborly. I told her I'd stop by and say, 'Hi,'" he explained.

Clayton forced a smile to his face, still worried that he might be bettered by his competitor.

"See you two tomorrow," Clayton said.

Randall and Joe left, and Clayton again pressed his intercom button.

"Sarah, get our backers on the phone. We need more money," Clayton said.

He walked around the desk, pushed his chair away, and peered out the window. In the distance, he saw the Imperial Records building. He had worked too hard to get where he was in life, and he wasn't about to let country's biggest hope slip through his fingers.

"We can't let Imperial get Randall," he muttered to himself.

Chapter Fifteen

On Nashville's Broadway Street, Joe and Randall opened the door to the Ernest Tubb Record Shop and melded into the throngs of people walking along the street. A musician's faded, light blue VW bus sat in a loading zone, and a man in a cowboy hat unloaded a couple of guitars and amps and placed them on the sidewalk. Music filled the air, slipping out of the opening and closing doors of the bars along the street.

"How's that for an impromptu autograph session?" Joe asked Randall as they continued their pace.

Just then, a buxom young woman with waist-length brunette hair exited the Record Shop and flashed a vivacious smile in their direction. Her curves moved with her as she fought against a form-fitting dress to catch up to them.

"Could you sign one more?" she asked breathlessly as she handed a 45 record to Randall.

Heads began to turn as passersby suddenly realized that the man who was to them a few minutes ago just another anonymous country music fan was actually a star.

"Sure, here you go," Randall said as he signed the 45 sleeve and handed it back.

"Just one more," the girl pleaded.

"What would you like me to sign?" Randall asked.

The girl opened the top of her dress slightly and indicated her chest. Randall's face turned red, and he began to stutter as he searched for a response.

"Well, uh … My pen hasn't got that much ink."

The girl laughed and ran off back to the store as a couple of other passersby handed him scraps of paper to sign.

"So, how's it feel to be a star?" Joe asked.

"Aw, I'm no star."

Three more people approached, pens and paper in hand.

"My friend," Joe said, "your life is about to change forever."

Randall looked up as a red 1965 Cadillac El Dorado convertible drove up the street. Its license plate read: "GEORGE."

"There goes a star, folks," Randall said, and as the people turned to look, Randall and Joe quickly stepped around the corner towards their less-than-classic ride.

"Unc, did you see who I saw?" Randall asked

"Yeah, that George Ritter is one fine artist," Joe said.

"No, I mean as we came around the corner, across the street I thought I saw Ray Raymond," Randall said. "Even looked like he had an arm in a sling."

"You're imagining things boy, just the worry getting to you. Pay it no mind," Joe said.

"OK," Randall said, "but it sure looked like Ray."

Chapter Sixteen

Grayson paced back and forth behind his desk in the Imperial Records tower office as he pressed his phone to his ear.

"Mr. Enrico, we have things in the works. Gaines has set up a meeting with Randall tonight at eight o'clock here at my office. We'll make sure he stops interfering with Billy Joe's single, yes, sir ... "

Outside in the reception area, Shelby Lee drummed her fingers impatiently. Grayson was already ten minutes late honoring their appointment, and she was beginning to wonder where her life was going to lead. It had started out well enough. At age nineteen, she won a talent contest in her hometown of Charleston, West Virginia, landing her a contract with a rival label.

Her first single, "Will You Be?" was a huge success, landing her enough fast cash to attract even more attention from her boyfriend, Tommy Reese, who had signed on as her manager.

Things began to take a turn for the worse though when her next song began to threaten Imperial's star Maybelle Mason. Grayson approached her, offered up some pipe dreams, and bought her contract. Then he sat on it. For the past year, she had been cooling her heels, waiting for a shot at Imperial he never intended to fire. It had been all she and Tommy could do to stretch the money they had to keep up appearances in Music City, let alone pay for groceries. She wanted answers. If nothing else, she wanted out.

"Have you told Mr. Grayson Shelby Lee is here?" Tommy asked Gloria, the receptionist.

A Badge or an Old Guitar

"He knows and will be with you as soon as he can," she said as a balding white man in his late twenties stormed into the reception area and made a beeline for Grayson's office.

Tommy returned to his seat and shook his head.

"I can't believe he is making you wait like this," he said.

Gloria rose quickly from her swivel chair. She was twice his age and more than twice as well-dressed. The man's long hair hung in strings from the bottom of a receding hairline, and she cringed as she thought how he seemed the type not to have slept in ages except perhaps on an afternoon when he accidentally nodded off on his desk.

Summoning her composure, she moved toward him. Bob Wilson was no stranger to the office, but he didn't come often. Bob worked as a song plugger, trying to get radio stations to play the latest songs that Imperial promoted.

"May I help you?" Gloria said.

"I'll go where I please!"

His boots stomped hurriedly toward the office door.

"Mr. Wilson, you can't go in there!"

Bob ignored her, opened the door, and walked up to Grayson, who was still on the phone. Seeing her efforts were in vain, Gloria reached for the doorknob and stood erect, waiting to usher the intruder back out again.

"I'm gonna kill you, you snake!" Bob said.

"Mr. Enrico, Bob Wilson just came in with some charts. Can I get back with you? Yes. Bye," Grayson said. He hung up the phone.

Chapter Seventeen

Joe and Randall eased up the hill by walking along the sidewalk towards the Ryman Auditorium.

Classic Country Star George Ritter walked around the corner to get in the Cadillac they spotted earlier. Randall approached George while Joe stood back and watched.

"Mr. Ritter, I'm J. Randall. I just wanted to tell you, your music has meant a lot to me," Randall said.

George turned and reached out his hand toward Randall.

"Thank you, son," George said.

While they shook hands, a rather plump lady in her fifties walked up to the duo, her blue and white print dress swishing as she moved.

"Could I have your autograph?" she asked with a grandmotherly smile.

"Sure," George said, without a moment of hesitation.

"No, not yours — his," the lady said, as she quickly reached in her purse and retrieved a slip of paper and a blue pen, which she handed to Randall.

Randall took the paper and signed it.

"Thank you!" she exclaimed as she walked away, smiling and giggling.

George chuckled at her elation, then turned his attention to Randall.

"So, you're this Randall I've been hearing about," George said.

"I guess so, sir," Randall said.

"Would you like to sit behind the wheel of my Josey?" George asked. Randall nodded and moved into the white leather driver's seat. George continued talking as Randall admired the pristine condition of the car's red dashboard and steering wheel.

"Son, you should be on top of the world. Everyone in Nashville has your name on their lips," George said.

Randall ran his hand across the leather seats.

"I'm just a police officer, Mr. Ritter, not a singer."

"You know what you just said to me about my music?" George asked.

"Yes, sir."

"One day, someone will come up to you and say the exact same thing. Son, a police officer helps hundreds of people each year. But there's only a chosen few with a talent like yours which can help millions with one song. For three minutes, you help them leave their problems behind, then they can face them with a better outlook," George said as Randall slid out of the driver's seat and stood beside him.

"Do you think I should be a singer?" Randall asked.

"Son, you are a singer. You've just got to believe in yourself."

George stepped into the car, placed the key in the ignition, and started the engine.

"Thank you," Randall said.

George reached his hand outside the car, and the two shook. Randall turned to join Joe.

"Say, Randall, that song of yours is the best I've heard in years. If you write another one like that and don't want it, send it to me," George said.

Randall and Joe watched the Cadillac grow small in the distance as George tapped the horn and waved out the window.

"Well, was he what you expected?" Joe asked.

"More. Even more," Randall said.

Suddenly, his expression changed.

"Did you see that?" Randall asked.

"What?" Joe asked.

"That looked like Ray Raymond's car."

"We need to get your mind on better things. How about seeing some more sights? There are some Civil War sites we can take in, and that Greek building, and how about the Opryland Hotel or Midnight Jamboree?" Joe asked.

Randall smiled.

"I'm along for the ride," he said.

"I think it's the other way around," replied Joe.

Chapter Eighteen

Cars surrounded the Nashville Palace, and its doors swung open and shut as customers moved in and out of the restaurant. Joe and Randall were seated in a booth across from each other, each with a plate of Southern fried chicken, green beans with chopped onions, and mashed potatoes smothered with white pepper gravy in front of them.

Opry star Janie Mae Ledford walked by the table. The Alabama native had been in Nashville since the 1960s when she started in Music City as a hairdresser before eventually rising to massive country stardom. Her string of hits included classics such as "Stay Away from My Man," "Your Heart Has Horns," and "Papa's Pears and Mama's Jars." After thirty years, she was considered a legend, often helping up-and-comers write their hits while touring annually on the country fair circuit and working the Opry.

"Are you two enjoying yourselves?" she said.

Joe came to his feet when he looked up and saw who spoke.

"Yes ma'am. I just love your singing," Joe said.

Randall quickly started to join him standing when Janie Mae reached over and placed her hand on his shoulder, stopping him in progress.

"And this cooking is not bad either," Randall added.

She motioned Joe to sit down.

"They use some of my recipes here. Y'all eat before it gets cold," she said. "Where are you boys from?"

"McKinney, Georgia, ma'am," Randall replied as he raised a chicken breast up and sunk his teeth into the meat.

"McKinney? I hear you have a new singing sensation from down there," Janie Mae said.

A smile lit up Joe's face as he looked across the table at Randall.

"We sure do. This is James Randall, Ms. Ledford. He's the singer you're talking about," Joe said.

She walked over and placed her hand on his shoulder again.

"My goodness, I sure like your sound," Janie Mae said. Randall blushed at the compliment, but it seemed to fill him with pride.

"Thank you, Ms. Ledford."

"I heard a little rumor about you at the Opry the other night," she said, quietly, leaning into Randall.

He widened his eyes in surprise.

"Rumor?"

"They really want you for the show."

"Me? On the Opry?"

"I told you your life was changing," Joe interjected.

Janie Mae stepped back from the table as she heard the band beginning to tune up on stage.

"I hope I see you there. Y'all have fun."

She headed toward backstage.

While Joe settled into their hotel for the evening, Randall assured him he would return as soon as he had fulfilled his promise to Elizabeth.

"Now is as good a time to do it as any," Randall had said. "We'll be able to get an early start the next day with that out of the way."

The streets were deserted in front of Imperial Records

as Randall pulled around into the parking lot and walked into the building. As he stepped inside the elevator, the ding for the seventh-floor button reverberated through the empty hallways.

"Feels like a ghost town," Randall muttered to himself as he walked into the empty waiting area. It was almost completely dark.

"That's odd," he muttered again. "Her business card said they were open until nine ..."

His leg bumped against a table.

"Ouch. Ms. Gaines, Ms. Gaines, are you here?"

Randall groped the wall for a lightswitch.

Suddenly, a figure dashed past him, dropping a small black gym bag before heading out the door. Randall whirled around, unable to make out who it was.

"Hey! Your bag!" Randall called.

He picked it up and walked towards Grayson's office and entered.

"Ms. Gaines! Ms. Gaines? Mr. Grayson?"

Then he saw it — Grayson lying on the floor, his eyes closed, his body lifeless. Randall reached down to feel full a pulse, and he sat the bag next to him on the floor. Suddenly, he was blinded by the overhead light turning on as two security guards entered the office.

"Freeze, Mister!" one of them commanded, as he pointed a gun at Randall.

Randall Franks

Chapter Nineteen

Randall, detained in the waiting room and awaiting questioning, caught glimpses of the officers searching Grayson's office for clues. Blue lights flashed in the darkness outside and reflected off the windows of the Imperial building, and yellow caution tape warned onlookers against entering the Imperial offices.

Patrick O'Shields, a detective in his late fifties, arrived, and stumbled over a carpet edge as he entered the waiting room. No one appeared to have caught his gaffe, so he quickly reclaimed his composure. He was an Irish-American old school detective who could have stepped out of an episode of Mannix. He came to Nashville from Chicago when his wife Roxie decided she could no longer stand the northern winters. The thought of finishing his police career in Florida was far from his desire, so when the opening in Nashville looked promising, he won a halfway compromise. He was now in his tenth year in Nashville and felt right at home.

"Well, what we've got here is an open and shut case. Right boys?" O'Shields said.

O'Shields noticed a female officer.

"And girls ... Mr. Randall, it seems you had the misfortune of being in the wrong place at the wrong time," he said.

Randall stood up.

"I'm glad someone believes me," he said.

"Believes you? I didn't say that. Let's see. I want to go over what appears to be the situation — a small town cop who is under suspension for assault ..."

Randall's jaw dropped.

"That's not exactly true, sir."

129

A Badge or an Old Guitar

O'Shields walked up to Randall and patted him on the shoulder.

"I know, I know, it was a misunderstanding."

Randall relaxed a bit.

"Yes, sir, my chief will verify that."

"Don't worry, son — I will verify it. Now, where was I? You were found in the office of one of our most powerful Music City citizens leaning over the body. By your side is a bag containing a pair of gloves and what appears to be the murder weapon — an antique dagger. Now all we need is a motive," O'Shields said.

Randall turned toward the wall and began to pace.

"You've got it all wrong. I was here to meet with Ms. Gaines," Randall said.

Just then, Elizabeth entered the room, her mouth open in apparent shock.

"Here she is now," Randall said.

O'Shields rushed over to comfort Elizabeth who had a look of panic on her face.

"Ms. Gaines, are you all right? Here, have a seat," O'Shields said.

"I'm fine," Elizabeth said. "I — I just didn't expect anything like this to happen."

O'Shields shifted back into detective mode.

"Could I ask you a few questions then?" O'Shields asked.

"Sure," she said as she noticed Randall standing at the end of the couch.

"Sorry I'm late, Randall. I was delayed in a meeting."

"You know Mr. Randall?" O'Shields asked.

"Of course. Mr. Grayson and I met him just before his

130

single went number one. 'Is There More to Life Than This?'" Elizabeth replied.

"Single? Is he a singer?" O'Shields asked.

"Randall is going to be the next Billy Joe," Elizabeth said.

O'Shields scoffed at her prediction.

"There's not much need for singing in jail," O'Shields said.

"What are you saying?" Elizabeth asked.

"We suspect Mr. Randall killed Mr. Grayson," O'Shields said.

Elizabeth laughed at the thought.

"Are you kidding? Mr. Eagle Scout here? I don't think so."

"All we need is a motive," O'Shields said.

Just then, Billy Joe entered the room.

"I think I may have one, detective," Billy Joe said.

"Who are you, sir?" O'Shields asked.

Billy Joe looked at O'Shields as if the detective had just informed him he had never made it past second grade.

"Detective," Elizabeth intervened, "this is Billy Joe." O'Shields was not impressed.

"Oh, forgive me. All you country singers look alike to me. If it's not Dorsey or Goodman I don't know it," O'Shields said. "So, what's the motive?"

"Grayson and Gaines here are meeting with Randall to sign him," Billy Joe replied.

"How is giving him a record deal a motive? That's a reason to keep him breathing," O'Shields said.

"No. No, they wouldn't have done anything with him.

A Badge or an Old Guitar

They would have sat on him until he was cold and my record was on top where it should be. Isn't that right, Elizabeth?"

She didn't answer. Randall cast her a disapproving glance.

"Is this true, Ms. Gaines?" O'Shields said.

She nodded her head yes.

"Now, there is a motive. I can just see the headline: 'Grayson Slain, Randall May Get More Than Life for This,'" O'Shields said.

Without missing a beat, he turned to Randall.

"You have the right to remain silent ..."

Chief Wilkes stood at the counter in the front squad room of the McKinney Police Station. He held a phone receiver in his hand. He was red in the face, and the veins in his neck popped out under his skin.

"Look, Detective, you've got the wrong man," the Chief said. "I don't care if it is an ironclad case. You've got the wrong man. Well, fine. Goodbye."

Will entered, carrying a newspaper.

"I can't believe that man is thinking Randall would murder Grayson," the chief said.

"It's just not him," Will agreed.

Will placed the newspaper on the desk. The headline read: "New Singing Star J. Randall Arrested for Murder."

The chief picked up the newspaper and without a pause slammed it down on the desk.

"Get me Joe Benton on the phone. I'll call in a few favors. Just maybe, with a little help, Randall can solve this case before he really sounds like Johnny Cash singing 'Folsom Prison Blues,'" he said.

Chapter Twenty

Nashville police officers moved in and out of the various rooms at headquarters while Joe and Randall walked down the hallway.

"Where did the bail money come from?" Randall asked.

"Well, I made a deal with Clayton Willows," Joe said. Randall's jaw dropped.

"You did what?"

"There's no obligation. He knows you won't skip. It's just a good-will gesture."

They arrived at the exit and saw a horde of press headed towards them.

"I don't think they have any good will on their minds. Let's find a back door," Randall said.

They saw another exit sign and ran.

Randall and Joe sat at a table inside Lottie's Diner.

"I don't understand why the chief wanted us to have help," Randall said.

Joe sat down a glass of sweet tea.

"Well he did, and right now we need it. He said we can't trust these folks," Joe said.

Right on cue, Jacob Marley, a fiftyish-looking man wearing a pinstripe suit, entered and walked up to their table.

"Gentlemen, the chief sent me. May I sit down?" he began.

Joe nodded.

"I'm Joe Benton. This is James Randall."

They shook hands.

"Well, I'm Jacob Marley, but everyone calls me

'Spirits.'"

"Spirits?" Joe questioned.

"It's a reference to Dickens' 'A Christmas Carol,' right?" Randall asked.

"No. I used to drink a lot. I don't anymore. Now, look, we are on a tight schedule here. So, let's get down to business. What do you need me to do?" Jacob said.

"The chief didn't tell you?" Randall asked.

"He said this was your … Well, he said it was your call," Jacob said.

"What is it you do, Spirits?" Randall asked.

"Let's just say I'm good at finding things. Information, items, whatever. Anything police can't. I'm a facilitator."

"You're a snitch?" Joe said.

"No, I'm a P.I. I understand we've got one more on this."

A beautiful woman in her late twenties entered the room. She was well-dressed, with a bit of a bookish appearance, and she had a brown leather briefcase in tow. She approached the table. Randall rose, and the others followed.

"Is one of you Sergeant James Randall?" she asked.

"That'd be me," Randall said.

"I'm here to help. I'm Ruby Ann Wilkes, your new attorney," she said.

"You're little Ruby, Chief's favorite niece!" Randall exclaimed. "Chief mentioned a few weeks ago you just passed the bar!"

"Sergeant Randall, I'm not here as the chief's niece. I'm here as your defense attorney," Ruby Ann said.

Joe leaned in to Randall and said, "And she's not so

little, neither."

"Miss Ruby Ann, this is Joe Benton and Jacob Marley — call him Spirits," Randall said.

"Hello," Ruby Ann said.

Everyone took a seat.

"OK, what's the plan?" Ruby Ann asked.

"The plan?" Randall echoed.

"Yes, the plan. How are we gonna prove your innocence?"

"I thought I was innocent until proven guilty."

"Is he kidding?" Ruby Ann said.

"Well, let's see. I guess we need to prove someone else's guilt. But who? Who would want to kill Grayson?" Randall said.

"An artist, or a backer, maybe an employee," Joe offered.

"Don't forget family, ex-wives, children," Jacob said.

"All good thoughts. Let's make a list," Randall said.

"Artist …" Randall said as the gears in his head began to turn. "I thought it was funny timing how Billy Joe turned up shortly after I found Grayson."

"Why would he want to kill him? Grayson made Billy Joe," Jacob said.

"Yeah, but Billy Joe was slipping with his latest project. Maybe he blamed Grayson," Joe said.

"OK, Joe, can you get an artist roster? Maybe Clayton has one. Let's find out if any were unhappy. Can you take care of that?" Randall asked.

"No problem," Joe said.

"Next, backers. Joe, where did the money come from?" Randall continued.

"I don't know," Joe said.

"West Coast investors," Jacob said.

"Sounds right up your alley, Spirits," Randall said.

"Yeah, I'm on it. Who are they? What do they do? The works," Jacob said.

"That leaves employees and family," Randall went on.

"Let me take the family. I'll have the other in no time," Jacob said.

"I doubt if they'll let me back in at Imperial to start asking questions," Randall said.

"They will if you're with me to examine the crime scene," Ruby Ann said.

"Well, maybe Ms. Gaines will help. She did defend me to the detective," Randall said.

"Just remember what Clayton said," Joe reminded him. "Don't trust her."

"Well, what are we doing sitting here?" Ruby Ann said. "Let's get going."

In an executive office at Imperial Records, Randall sat by Ruby Ann as his new-found attorney directed the conversation.

"So, Ms. Gaines, you believe my client is innocent?" Elizabeth nodded.

"That boy scout wouldn't hurt a fly."

"So, who do you think wanted Grayson dead?" Randall asked.

"Who didn't? Be real. This is a man who wasn't loved. Anyone who knew him could have and would have killed him," Elizabeth said.

'We would welcome a more specific suggestion," Ruby Ann said.

"Ms. Gaines, could just anyone enter the building?" Randall asked.

"No. It had to be someone on our clearance list, an employee or an artist," Elizabeth said.

"Could we have a copy of your clearance list for that day as well as an employee list?" Ruby Ann asked.

"I'll have security give you everything you need," Elizabeth said.

"Ms. Gaines, if one person wanted Grayson dead more than anyone else, who would it be?" Randall asked.

"Other than me? Billy Joe. Grayson was stealing him blind. He discovered a few weeks ago when he found out if the new project didn't fly, he was out," Elizabeth said.

"Stealing, how?" Randall asked.

"Nothing illegal. It was all through contracts Billy Joe signed with Grayson when he started," Elizabeth said.

"Why didn't he leave?" Ruby Ann asked.

"He couldn't. No other company could touch him. The contracts had him all tied up as long as Grayson held them," Elizabeth said.

"So, with Grayson gone, the contracts … ?" Elizabeth pressed.

"Null and void. They were exclusive to Grayson. We're still trying to figure out whether he's still under contract to Imperial," Elizabeth said.

"Thank you, Ms. Gaines. You've been very helpful," Randall said.

Ruby Ann and Randall stood and began to leave.

"One more thing, Ms. Gaines," Randall said. "When you were late, you said you were detained by a meeting. With whom?"

A Badge or an Old Guitar

"Why, sergeant, does this mean you suspect me?" she said. "I was meeting with our radio promotion man, Bob Wilson."

"Thank you," Randall replied.

Randall Franks

Chapter Twenty One

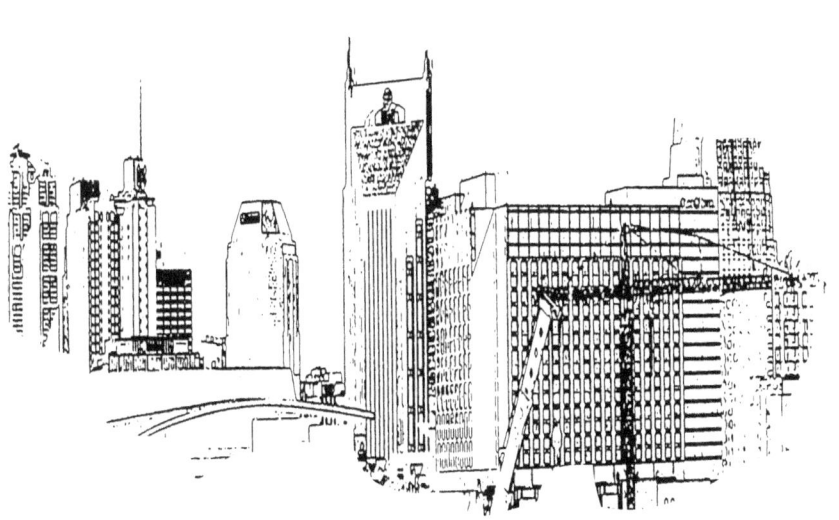

Joe and Clayton exited Lottie's Diner and walked towards the parking lot.

"I tell you Joe — it was probably Elizabeth Gaines. With Grayson out of the way, she's in line to take over," Clayton said.

"Would there be anyone else? Any of the artists on the roster?" Joe asked.

"He did sign an act just to sit on it," Clayton said.

"Which one is that?" Joe asked.

Clayton looked at the list.

"The last one on the list ... Shelby Lee. She was too close to overtaking his girl star," Clayton said.

"So, do you think she could have ..." Joe trailed off.

"She probably didn't, but she has a rather interesting boyfriend named Tommy Reese who would likely not be too happy about losing his meal ticket," Clayton said.

"How do you know so much about them?" Joe returned.

"Grayson stole her from me," Clayton said.

"Did Grayson have any vices?" Joe asked.

"Just all the money he spent on those Civil War relics he collected. He spent more on them than on his artists or ex-wives," Clayton said.

Cars passed swiftly in front of the Union Station Hotel. Randall and Ruby Ann sat in the lobby, waiting, as Jacob arrived.

"You will never believe what I found out," Jacob said. Joe arrived elated.

"You won't believe it," Joe said.

Jacob spoke up.

"I was here first," Jacob said.

Before they came to a friendly debate, Ruby Ann interceded.

"Guys, let's hear it," she said, as she clapped her palms together.

The bellhop got Randall's attention and pointed out Bob Wilson.

"You sort all this out, Ruby Ann. It looks like Mr. Wilson is here. I'll talk with him," Randall said.

Randall followed and reached the elevator just in time to get on as the door closed. Bob tapped a button to send them to the sixth floor.

He and Randall were the only two passengers.

"Mr. Wilson, I'm Sergeant James," Randall said.

Bob didn't waste any time.

"Look, I don't know anything," he said.

"I just wanted to ask you about Mr. Grayson," Randall said.

"That rat, I'm glad he's dead. Because of him I'm staying here. He told my wife I was having an affair," Bob said.

"Were you?" Randall asked.

"Yes, but there was no reason. He had me fired because I wasn't doing a good job with Billy Joe's single. I was! Next week he'll be back above you," Bob said.

As they reached the fifth floor, the elevator door opened. No one got on. It began to close.

"Yes, well. Did you have a meeting with Elizabeth Gaines the night of the murder?" Randall continued.

As the door closed, a gun fired, killing Bob Wilson. The gun fell to the floor inside the elevator as the door shut. Randall tried to open the door by hitting several buttons, but the elevator was already continuing on to the sixth floor. He leaned over and checked Bob's pulse.

At last, the door opened on the sixth floor to reveal a woman waiting her turn. Seeing Bob on the floor bleeding, she began screaming for help while Randall ran past her. Seeing no one in the hall, he ran down the stairs to the fifth floor.

In the hotel lobby, the elevator where Bob lay stood open as police searched for clues. A door to the stairwell nearby opened and out stepped Randall, who had just returned after searching each floor all the way down for anyone who could be the shooter.

"That's him, he's the man," the woman said.

O'Shields entered just in time for this revelation.

"My, record executives drop like flies around you, Randall. You won't get out on bail this time. A murder weapon, a witness seeing you flee the scene," O'Shields said.

O'Shields' men placed handcuffs on Randall.

"Where are you taking my client? He's out on bail," Ruby Ann said.

"Not anymore," O'Shields replied. "He's under arrest for the murder of Bob Wilson."

Ruby Ann and Randall sat and talked in a police interrogation room at Nashville Police headquarters.

"If you get me out of here, I'm going back to McKinney to be a police officer. I'd much rather put the bad guys in than be one," Randall said.

A Badge or an Old Guitar

"You're not the bad guy here, Randall," Ruby Ann said.

"So what did Unc and Jacob find out?" Randall asked.

"Well, apparently Grayson was backed by some shady characters in Los Angeles — a man named Enrico leads the investors," Ruby Ann said.

"Enrico, is he a crime boss?" Randall asked.

"Maybe, but he's clean. No charges, no convictions. Joe said the word was the investors were unhappy about Billy Joe's poor performance. Joe also said that we should look hard at Gaines; with Grayson out of the picture she takes control," Ruby Ann said.

"She was supposedly meeting with Wilson. How convenient that he died before confirming her alibi," Randall mused.

"Or not confirming it," Ruby Ann added.

"Any other suspects?" Randall asked.

"Joe mentioned another artist named Shelby Lee," she said.

"Somebody checking her out?" he asked.

"Jacob," she replied.

"What about family?" he asked.

"Jacob really came through. Three ex-wives, no kids, no insurance, and what he has goes to his mother. No motives," she said.

"Well, one thing's for sure. I'm here for the duration, so you three will have to flush out the real killer," Randall said.

"And how do we do that?" she asked.

Randall's eyes met hers with a look of confidence as he replied.

"You just need a good dog."

Randall Franks

Chapter Twenty Two

In a rented sedan, Jacob drove up to a sprawling antebellum mansion. Horses galloped across the green fields that led up to the main house as he pulled up to the speaker at the security gate.

Jacob was dressed like a hood from the 1930s — brimmed hat, suit, white and black shoes. He pressed the intercom button.

"Yeah," a man said over the intercom.

"This is Vincenso. I'm here to see Billy Joe," Jacob said.

"Billy Joe doesn't know you."

"Mr. Enrico sent me."

The gate opened, and Jacob drove toward the house. Jacob walked down some stairs between large lion statues toward the pool.

Billy Joe sat with two beautiful girls in bikinis. Jacob approached and sat.

"Mr. Billy Joe, it is a pleasure to meet you. I love your music," Jacob said.

"So, what does Mr. Enrico want? I've tried to reach him," Billy Joe said.

"He is very unhappy about these deaths, Billy Joe. You see, this press, the police, it's not good for business."

"What are you talking about? My CD is rising. All the press is selling CDs like hotcakes."

"Not your business — Mr. Enrico's business. You see, he doesn't like all the questions. He would like to see you tonight at nine. You know the warehouse at 12th and Railroad? Be there."

"Why does he want to see me?"

"He just wants to deal with all of this."

Jacob rose to his feet.

"See you, Mr. Billy Joe," he called over his shoulder.

Jacob drove into the parking lot of Lottie's Diner. Still wearing his suit and hat, Jacob entered the diner.

Ruby Ann and Joe sat in a booth.

"Well, how'd it go, Spirits?" Joe began.

"Billy Joe should be there," Jacob answered.

"How is Enrico going to feel about this if he finds out?" Ruby Ann asked.

"Word is, he's out of the country for the next few weeks. So, we can only hope he doesn't," Jacob said.

"So, what's the next step?" Ruby Ann asked.

"Vincenso places a call to Elizabeth Gaines. All we need now is a limo and someone to play Mr. Enrico," Jacob said.

Ruby Ann and Jacob looked at Joe.

"What? Who me? No, I can't," Joe said.

"They won't see you; you'll be in the car. Jacob will be wired and he'll have a cellphone. You will just drive up as a presence," Ruby Ann said.

"You really think one of them will admit they did it?" Joe asked.

"Maybe not, but what they do afterwards will tell the tale," Jacob said.

"Spirits, did you have any luck on Shelby Lee?" Ruby Ann continued.

"Nothing. She and her boyfriend seem to have dropped off the earth, but I've got some feelers out."

"Now I better see what I can do about getting Sergeant Randall out of jail," Ruby Ann said.

"He's getting another bail hearing?" Joe asked.

"Tomorrow," she said.

"Any chance?" Joe asked.

Jacob interjected: "Is the moon made of cheese?"

Ruby Ann heaved a sigh of frustration from her apartment building towering above Nashville's music scene. She flipped through a stack of law books on a table as the phone rang.

"Uncle, you always know when to call," she said. Chief Wilkes sat in his office in the McKinney Police Station.

"Oh, Ruby, what's bothering you?"

"Uncle, I just don't know if I can do this."

"It's the case, isn't it?"

"Uncle, it was bad enough with one murder. Now it's two. I can't even hope to get him out on bail again."

"Is there a chance of finding another suspect?"

"We are all working on it, but I don't know."

"Ruby, is Sergeant Randall innocent?"

"Of course he is!"

The chief was silent for several seconds before he spoke.

"Do you think the evidence will put him in jail?"

"Yes, Uncle, I do."

"Then I would be looking at ways to distance him from the evidence, work on getting some of it thrown out."

"I've thought of that. I've just not found a way yet. Thanks, Uncle Roy."

"Call me if you need me."

"I will."

A Badge or an Old Guitar

Ruby Ann set the phone in its cradle and began flipping through her books once more.

Chapter Twenty Three

Jacob stood just outside his car inside an abandoned warehouse. Elizabeth's car arrived, followed by Billy Joe's truck. They both got out.

"OK, We're here. Where is Mr. Enrico?" Elizabeth asked.

"Patience," Jacob replied.

Jacob placed a call on a mobile phone. A black limo pulled up. The windows were tinted dark and obscured any view to the inside. A back window lowered slightly. Jacob walked over.

"Yes, Mr. Enrico," Jacob said.

The window closed.

"What's going on?" Billy Joe asked.

Jacob opened his coat. A gun was visible. His phone rang. He answered.

Both Elizabeth and Billy Joe seemed nervous and unsure about the situation.

"Yes, sir. As I was saying, Mr. Enrico is very unhappy about what's happening with this Grayson and Wilson business," Jacob said.

"I didn't have anything to do with their deaths," Elizabeth said.

"Neither did I," Billy Joe said.

"Mr. Enrico is well aware of what happened. There's no need to talk about it. I'm just here to clean up a few things," Jacob said.

Jacob took out his gun.

"I tell you, I didn't have anything to do with it. If it was anyone, it was Billy Joe," Elizabeth said.

"Me? I may have wanted him dead, but I didn't kill him!" Billy Joe retorted.

The phone rang again.

"Yes, sir, I'll finish it," Jacob said.

The limo drove away.

"Where's he going?" Elizabeth asked.

"He hates blood," Jacob said.

"Look, mister, I don't want to die. I'm worth a lot of money. How much do you want? I won't even say anything about whatever you do to her," Billy Joe said.

"You, ungrateful, pompous … !" Elizabeth exclaimed.

"Enough," Jacob interrupted. "Look, you both live or you both don't. Now … I believe you, that you didn't kill Grayson or Wilson. Mr. Enrico has left this in my hands. So, I'm going to grant you both a stay. If the police get the real killer before I do, then neither of you has a thing to worry about," Jacob said.

"Thank you. Can we go?" Billy Joe asked.

"Yes."

Billy Joe and Elizabeth both left. Jacob picked up the phone and dialed.

"Release the hounds," Jacob said.

Elizabeth's car pulled out and turned right. A car driven by Joe fell in behind her. Billy Joe's truck took the opposite direction. Ruby Ann fell in behind and followed.

Elizabeth pulled into the parking lot of Imperial Records. Joe pulled up across the street.

As she got out of the car, Tommy walked up to her and began shouting. Joe walked closer to try to hear, but the conversation finished just as he got within earshot. No sooner had Elizabeth handed Tommy some money did the scene break up, as she went inside and picked up her mobile phone.

Billy Joe's truck went by, then Ruby Ann's car. Ruby Ann was on the phone inside her car.

"He looks like he's headed to his house. But I'll stay on him. Have Jacob meet me there. Wait a minute," Ruby Ann said.

They both changed direction.

"Looks like he's headed somewhere else. Why don't you have Jacob pick up on Ms. Gaines?

When I get a positive location I'll call and you can meet me," she said.

"We have a third player, I haven't seen him before. Early twenties, looks like a football player," Joe said. "He already left after she gave him some money."

"Sounds like Tommy Reese. Maybe we can track him down," Ruby Ann said.

Joe still sat in his car with a phone to his ear.

"I'll talk to you soon — Ms. Gaines is on the move," Joe said.

He hung up and watched Elizabeth as she walked over to her car with a suitcase.

She started the engine and pulled out. Joe picked up his phone again.

"Spirits? Yeah, it looks like Ms. Gaines is our man. She's packed a bag and looks like she's headed to the bus station."

Jacob's car was moving through Nashville's streets in pursuit.

"The bus station?" Jacob echoed. "That's not her style. She would fly or drive. Keep on her, I'll meet you there."

A Badge or an Old Guitar

Nashville Bus Station was busy in the middle of night. Elizabeth pulled around and parked. Joe stopped and got out to follow.

Joe caught up with Elizabeth as she passed the ticket counter and headed toward the lockers. She placed the bag inside one, took the key, and stepped into the rest-room. Jacob walked up to Joe.

"Looks like she's trying to hide something in the lockers. She's stepped into the bathroom," Joe said.

"Well, maybe she's not leaving then," Jacob returned.

"No, Ms. Wilkes wanted me to take over for her," Joe said.

"Why don't you get going? I'll keep an eye on Ms. Gaines. How long has she been in that bathroom?" Jacob said.

"It's been a while," Joe replied.

"Watch the door. I'm gonna check for her car," Jacob said.

Jacob left then looked out a window.

"Joe, she's gone. You meet Ms. Wilkes. I'll see if Ms. Gaines is headed home," Jacob said.

"How did she see me?" Joe muttered.

"Just go. We'll figure that out later," Jacob said.

Chapter
Twenty Four

People bustled in and out of the Davidson County Courthouse.

Judge Miriam Lester, a stoic woman in her fifties, was on the bench. Judge Lester was elected to the bench after years as a prosecutor and though she was fair, she tended to look more kindly on the side from whence she came. She sat strongly with the conviction that she was bigger than life even though she was only five-feet, two-inches tall.

Assistant District Attorney Jack Stevens, a balding man in his late thirties, stood in a poorly tailored blue suit looking through his thick reading glasses at some notes on the prosecution table. Ruby Ann and Randall stood behind the defense table. A bailiff, a court reporter, and a half dozen people in the gallery looked on.

"Mr. Randall, how do you plead?" the judge began.

"Not guilty, Your Honor."

"What about bail, Mr. Stevens?" he asked.

Ruby Ann leaned in to Randall.

"Let me do the talking," she reminded him.

"Your Honor, Mr. Randall was out on bail when arrested for this crime," Stevens said. "The people feel there should be no bail."

Randall opened his mouth to protest, but Ruby Ann calmed him with a touch and spoke up.

"Your Honor, Sergeant Randall is not a flight risk," she said. "He is a qualified officer at the McKinney Police Department where he has proudly served his community for nearly twenty years. He is currently on leave and exploring a different career path."

A Badge or an Old Guitar

Stevens countered, "Your Honor, this man is accused of killing two of Music City's leading citizens."

"Your Honor, my client was a witness to a shooting, and as a trained officer was chasing a fleeing suspect," Ruby Ann quickly interjected.

The judge called a halt to the rapid fire arguments.

"Mr. Stevens, Ms. Wilkes, we are not here to argue this case. We are trying to decide if there should be bail. Mr. Stevens, has this man been convicted of any crimes?"

"No, Your Honor. But that leave mentioned by Ms. Wilkes is not voluntary. The defendant is currently suspended over an incident where he broke a man's arm inside his own chief's office," Stevens said.

"Is this true, Ms. Wilkes? Did your client break a man's arm?" Judge Lester asked.

Ruby Ann had discussed the incident with her uncle prior to taking the case, and she responded with confidence.

"Your honor, Sergeant Randall was protecting a youth, and while trying to restrain a parent out of control with anger, there was a scuffle, and the man fell and broke his arm. The sergeant was suspended during the review process, as is standard procedure. His chief was present and was a witness to the incident and I feel he would testify to the accidental nature of it."

"Thank you all. Bail is set at $100,000. Next case," the judge said.

Randall closed his eyes for a minute, and he heaved a small sigh of relief.

"I'll work on getting bail money," Ruby Ann said.

"Make sure Jacob and Unc stay on the foxes," Randall said.

The bailiff led Randall away.

"Where will we get that kind of money?" Ruby Ann said to herself.

Ruby Ann came out of the courtroom and walked down the hallway. A clerk walked up to her.

"Ms. Wilkes, I need your signature on these papers. You can take Mr. Randall with you," the clerk said.

"What about the bail money?" Ruby Ann asked.

"It's all been taken care of," the clerk said.

"By whom?" Ruby Ann asked.

"I don't know. All I know is it's taken care of," the clerk said.

Randall walked quickly.

"That was fast," Randall said.

"A little too fast," Ruby Ann said.

Jacob walked up.

"So, how's the chase?" Randall asked.

"Well, Billy Joe is in sight, but we've lost Ms. Gaines completely after she dropped off a suitcase at the bus locker," Jacob said.

The three walked out of the building.

"I wonder what's in the suitcase," Randall said.

"Money or documents. Proof of something to protect her," Jacob said.

Jacob and Ruby Ann walked out with Randall following.

"Well, I would have never expected Gaines to be the murderer. In fact, the person who ran into me was much larger," Randall said.

"It would help to know what's in that suitcase," Ruby Ann said.

A Badge or an Old Guitar

"Who came up with the money for bail? Did Unc get it from Clayton again?" Randall asked.

"Joe couldn't have. I don't know who did it," Ruby Ann said.

"Some good news, Randall, you were voted fans' favorite new star at the Fan Awards last night," Jacob said.

"You're kidding," Randall said.

Just then, a gun fired in their direction. All three went down.

Randall Franks

Chapter Twenty Five

Detective O'Shields, Randall, Jacob, and Ruby Ann sat inside O'Shields' office at Nashville Police Headquarters. Through the windows, the squad room was filled with the bustle of a busy force. Sergeant Braxton, an African-American in his mid-thirties, stood near the door.

"You're telling me that whoever was shooting at you probably killed Grayson and Wilson," O'Shields said.

"That's it, exactly," Randall said.

"What do any of these incidents have to do with one another except for one common element — you?" O'Shields said.

"Detective, someone bailed Sergeant Randall out to take a shot at him," Ruby Ann said.

"So, he has some enemies. What cop doesn't?"

"Enemies? Detective, I've had a few folks with their noses out of joint who object to how I did my job, but the only enemy is maybe Judson Deavers," Randall said.

"See? What did I tell you? So, why did this Judson… " O'Shields paused, trying to remember his last name.

"Deavers," Randall said.

"… Deavers consider you an enemy?"

"Well, I took his cat's eye."

"See, he took his cat's eye," O'Shields said. " … You took his what?"

"It was fair and square. I beat him for it."

"So, you beat him up?"

"I sure did. Up one side and down the other!"

"See, there's no telling how many people would want to take a shot at him," O'Shields said.

"I don't think Judson would take a shot at me over such a thing," Randall said.

"Why not? You beat him, didn't you?"

"Sure, but somebody always gets beat in a good game of marbles! Besides, I let him win the cat's eye back next time we played."

"Marbles? Ohh ...."

"Can't you just concede that maybe there's more to these cases than meets the eye?" Ruby Ann said.

"Now, don't you start this eye business," O'Shields said.

"What about Ms. Gaines? We still don't know where she is," Jacob said.

"And what business is it of yours?" O'Shields asked.

"Mr. Marley works for me. And since your department seems content putting an innocent man in jail, we're having to do your job," Ruby Ann said.

"Ms. Wilkes, in my opinion, Mr. Randall is guilty. But you are right, the shooting does add a new ingredient to the mix. I'll have my men stir the pot a bit, see what comes to the surface," O'Shields said.

"Thank you, Detective," Randall said.

O'Shields' eyes met Randall's.

"You — keep out of trouble. No more bodies," O'Shields said.

"Yes, sir."

Everyone left except O'Shields and the sergeant.

"Sergeant, let's get some men out and find Ms. Gaines," O'Shields said.

"Detective, you're not falling for Simple Simon's con game?" Braxton said.

"No, sergeant. I just don't like holes. With this shooting and Ms. Gaines taking off, that leaves some big ones.

When we put Randall in jail, I want to make sure he stays. Find out who did the shooting," O'Shields said.

"We've already canvassed the area," Braxton said.

"Do it again, and again, and again, until you find what I need."

"Yes, sir."

Chapter
Twenty Six

At the Jentry Bond Company, Ruby Ann and Randall walked up to a desk where an East Indian woman stood behind the service counter.

"May I be of service?" she asked in a thick accent.

"Hello. I'm Ruby Ann Wilkes. This is James Randall. Your company just made bail for Mr. Randall. Could we find out who arranged for it?" Ruby Ann asked.

"Just a moment," the woman replied.

She pulled a file.

"Yes, here is his file ... Oh, I see. I see ... Hmm ... yes, now I see," she said as she looked over the documents.

"What do you see?" Randall asked.

"I can't tell you."

"My client has a right to know," Ruby Ann said.

"Yes, he does —and if I knew, I'd tell him."

"You don't know?" Ruby Ann asked.

"No, there's nothing in the file."

"Thank you," Ruby Ann said.

Ruby Ann drummed her fingers on the counter in semi-stifled exasperation, then she and Randall left.

"One thing about it, somebody wanted you out," Ruby Ann said.

"But who? Who?" Randall said.

As they got in their convertible, across the street in the front of a parking lot, a limo pulled up and stopped. The rear windows were open. A man's hand and suit jacket were visible. Randall and Ruby Ann got in and took off in the convertible. The hand motioned to a car parked a few spaces behind the convertible on the street to follow, the window closed, and the limo pulled out in the opposite direction.

A Badge or an Old Guitar

Joe sat in his car outside Billy Joe's girlfriend's apartment. Jacob pulled up, walked up, and got in.

"Any sign of movement?" Jacob asked.

"Nothing," Joe said.

"Well, let's leave Billy Joe on his own. We have bigger fish to fry," Jacob said.

"I don't think he's going anywhere," Joe said.

"If he's not gone by now, he's not our man anyway. We got to meet Randall and Ms. Wilkes at the restaurant," Jacob said.

Randall, Ruby Ann, Jacob, and Joe sat around the table at Lottie's Diner.

"It must be Ms. Gaines. Billy Joe didn't run except to his girl," Jacob said.

"Do we have any other possibilities?" Randall asked. "Maybe we caught someone else in the trap and didn't even know it."

"Maybe Ms. Gaines has a boyfriend," Joe said.

"I doubt it. She's the type who marries her work," Ruby Ann said.

"Well, we shook someone up enough to want me dead. What about the real Enrico? Any sign of him?" Randall asked.

"My people tell me he's still out of the country," Jacob said.

"What about some of the other artists?" Joe said.

"How about that girl singer?" Randall asked. "What was her name?"

"Shelby Lee. She's not been seen," Joe said. "But Ruby Ann said she thought the man I saw with Elizabeth may have been her manager, Tommy."

"Maybe no one put out the right bait," Randall said.

"Bait? Does everything have to be about hunting or fishing to you?" Ruby Ann said.

"Isn't it?" Randall replied. "Jacob, see if you can dig up any more on Wilson and this Tommy. Maybe we can find a lead there. Ruby Ann, check in with the detective and see if they've made progress on Ms. Gaines. Unc, you and I have a little fishing to do."

"I've got my pole in the trunk," Joe said.

Ruby Ann's mobile phone rang as she drove the convertible through town.

"Hi, Ruby. How are you doing?" said the chief, calling from his office in McKinney.

"Uncle, much better. We've got the police looking into things now."

"That's great. I knew you could do it."

"It wasn't me. It was a sniper who took a shot at Sergeant Randall."

"A shot? Is he all right?"

"Oh, sure. He's fine. I'm on my way over to see if the detective has found anything yet."

"Keep up the good work. Give Sergeant Randall my best. Oh! Tell him everything has been worked out down here. His job is waiting on him."

"That's great, Uncle. I'll see you."

Randall and Joe walked out into the light of day in front of Superior Records as they talked.

"It's nice of Clayton to help us with the plan," Joe said.

"Do you think it will work?"

"It will be like a bear finding a beehive. She won't be able to resist," Randall said.

"OK. Where to now?" Joe asked.

"Let's see if we can find Spirits," Randall said.

As they walked by, they noticed the limo they saw earlier.

Detective O'Shields walked to his car outside Nashville Police Headquarters as Ruby Ann caught up with him.

"Detective!" Ruby Ann said.

"Ms. Wilkes, hello. You'll have to excuse me. I have to check out a lead," O'Shields said.

"On Ms. Gaines?"

"Ms. Wilkes, leave the police work to us."

"Have you found anything on Ms. Gaines, Detective?" Ruby Ann persisted.

"Not yet, but we think she may have some relatives in town."

"Relatives?"

"A sister. We haven't found her yet, but we will."

"Thank you, Detective."

O'Shields climbed in his car and drove away.

Jacob stood outside a café near Music Row and talked with a man who wore gold-framed sunglasses and a brown cowboy hat with a gold leather band. Randall and Joe walked up.

"Thanks, Stixs," Jacob said.

"Anything on Wilson?" Randall asked.

"You won't believe this. After his wife dumped him, Wilson dumped his mistress, and she wasn't a happy camper. They had a big fight at the Playback Club," Jacob said.

"Do you think she could have killed him?" Joe asked.

"Or was it his wife?" Randall said. "He had two women scorned to deal with. Or it could still be Ms. Gaines."

"It's hard to say, but if you ask me, it was the girl-friend," Jacob said. "An ex-wife can make you pay for years. Death would be too quick and easy."

"In any event, let's see whether we can find more on the wife and girlfriend," Randall said.

"I'm on it," Jacob said.

"Anything on Tommy and Shelby?" Randall asked.

"I hear they are staying in one of the dive motels on the south side of town," Jacob said. "I am headed out that way to see if I can find any leads."

Ruby Ann talked to someone as she drove up, cell phone to her ear.

"That's great, let me write that down," Ruby Ann said.

She pulled out a date book and wrote down an address. Randall, Jacob, and Joe walked over to the car.

"Thank you," Ruby Ann said into the phone. She hung up, then turned to the others. "Guess what?"

"You found a new singer," Randall said.

"Detective O'Shields said Ms. Gaines has a sister in town, but they haven't found her yet," Ruby Ann said.

"Why so excited?" Joe asked.

"I've got her address. I'll bet we find Ms. Gaines there," Ruby Ann said.

"That's great. Why don't you and I check it out?" Randall said. "Give Unc the address and he can go bring Detective O'Shields to meet us."

"I better work on the Wilson girls. I might scare Ms. Gaines anyway," Jacob joked.

"I hear you have that effect on all the women," Ruby Ann said.

"OK, let's get going," Randall said.

Randall hopped in the car. As it made a U-turn and drove away, the limo followed.

Randall and Ruby Ann stood at an apartment door with no peep hole and knocked. A voice called from behind the door. It belonged to Elizabeth.

"Who is it?" she asked.

"Pizza delivery," Randall said.

The door opened, and there stood Elizabeth. She began to slam the door.

"Ms. Gaines, could we please speak with you?" Randall asked.

Reluctantly, Elizabeth stopped, opened the door, and motioned them in.

"I hope you both understand my reservations," she said.

"Not really, Ms. Gaines," Ruby Ann said. "You disappeared. The police are looking for you."

"The police?"

"Your sudden disappearance made them suspicious that maybe you did have something to do with the murders," Randall said.

"The murders … No … I'm just hiding."

"Hiding from what, Ms. Gaines?" Randall asked.

"Or is it from whom?" Ruby Ann said.

"In the entertainment business, it takes a lot of money to make a star. Sometimes you work for companies never knowing where the money comes from. When Grayson died, I was left in charge — in charge of a lot of money. I'm afraid," Elizabeth said.

"Of losing the money?" Ruby Ann pressed.

"No. No, I'm afraid of the investor. He might … I'm afraid he might kill me," Elizabeth said.

No sooner had the words left her mouth did the door open and three men enter. Two looked like enforcers in suits. The third spoke.

"We don't kill people anymore — at least not so you'd notice," he said.

Randall Franks

Chapter Twenty Seven

Randall stood with Elizabeth and Ruby Ann slightly behind him as he faced off the man and his enforcers.

"Mr. Enrico, I presume?" Randall said.

"Very good for a local yocal. This is my personal trainer, Otto …"

Randall eyed the burly man in black.

"Personal trainer, indeed," he muttered under his breath.

"… And this is my attorney, Mr. Sims," Enrico continued, gesturing toward the man standing with his arms crossed, a menacing look on his face.

"I want to thank you and Ms. Wilkes for leading us to Ms. Gaines," Enrico said.

"Us?" Randall asked.

"We knew if we stuck with you, you'd find her. There is no one more resourceful than a man headed for the chair. Now, Ms. Gaines, where is the money, and where are the contracts? We've searched the office, Grayson's house, and your apartment. So, the only place left is with you," Enrico said.

"If I know where it is, and I tell you, you won't hurt me?" Elizabeth asked, her voice shaking.

"There's a better chance of being hurt if you don't tell," Enrico said impatiently. "Where is it?"

Elizabeth pulled a key from her pocket.

"Here. Number seventeen at the bus station. Everything is there."

"I'm glad you see things our way. Now, we're all gonna take a little trip," Enrico said.

"How 'bout I go? Leave the ladies," Randall said.

"We all will go to the bus station and if the money's

there, we all go our separate ways," Enrico said.

Before they could leave, the ajar door opened. Detective O'Shields entered with two officers, guns drawn. Joe was right behind them.

"And where are we all going?" O'Shields said coolly.

"Detective, am I glad to see you!" Randall exclaimed.

"I'm glad there are no new bodies lying around, Randall. So, where are we going?" O'Shields said again.

"These gentlemen were going to take us for a ride — to the bus station, to get some money out of a locker," Ruby Ann said.

"Well, why don't we all take a ride — to the police station — and I'll just have the money meet us there? Let's go, gentlemen and ladies," O'Shields said.

Randall and Ruby Ann were seated in O'Shields office, and he entered.

"I believe I've got everything sorted out," O'Shields said.

"So, did Ms. Gaines kill Grayson?" Randall asked.

"What? ... No, not that. We've got a half million in cash which seems to be legitimate. An investment banker who likes to play act that he's a mobster."

"He's not?" Ruby Ann asked.

"No."

"What about his two gorillas?" Randall asked.

"A lawyer and a personal trainer ..."

"Really?" Ruby Ann said.

"They don't even carry guns," O'Shields said.

"How is Ms. Gaines?" Randall asked.

"Fine, except she keeps mentioning some guy named

Vincenso that nobody's heard of," O'Shields said.

"So, does this put us any closer to clearing me?" Randall asked.

"Actually, it just strengthens our case. Finding Ms. Gaines just puts you a little closer to the slammer," O'Shields said.

"Thank you for your help, Detective. We'll be going," Ruby Ann said.

"Thanks, Detective," Randall said.

"Randall, I still think you're guilty," O'Shields said. "No more bodies."

Jacob stood in the living room of a well-decorated middle-class home as he spoke to Rita Wilson, who was seated on a plush brown couch.

"Ms. Wilson, I want to thank you for seeing me ...You've been very helpful," Jacob said.

Rita rose.

"That's quite all right, Mr. Marley. If it helps that nice singer Randall, I'm all for it. He's kinda cute. I'll show you to the door."

"One more thing, Ms. Wilson. Where were you the afternoon of your husband's death?" Jacob asked.

"Why, Mr. Marley, do you suspect me?"

"Just routine, Ms. Wilson."

"I was playing golf at the Hudson Club all day. My foursome can verify that."

"Thank you, Ms. Wilson."

Jacob left and headed down on the south of the city. One of his informants suggested checking out a cheap place out in the boonies. As he pulled across from the

185

motel, he looked up and realized that Tommy had walked out of a rural convenience store he was parked next to; he carried a small bag of groceries. He stopped and looked at the paper box. He saw the headline, "Superior searches for Shelby Lee." He set the groceries down and hunted a quarter. Not finding one, he forced the box open and took a paper.

Jacob watched as Tommy took the newspaper, walked across the road, and entered room six at the Dixie Breeze Travel Lodge. Then Jacob drove back toward the city.

Randall and Ruby Ann sat alone at a table at a restaurant.

"I want to be completely honest, Sergeant Randall," Ruby Ann said.

"Please, call me James," Randall said as he looked deeply into her brown eyes.

Ruby Ann blushed under his gaze but turned her attention back to the case.

"James, I just don't see a way out of this one. I don't think we are going to be able to beat these charges," she said.

"Ms. Wilkes ..."

"Ruby Ann," she interjected.

"Ruby Ann ... I know you're doing your best. So are Joe and Jacob. Something will break."

"By tomorrow at two ... We have to be in court and we have absolutely nothing."

"Don't worry, Ruby Ann ... God hasn't brought us this far for nothing. We'll make it."

Randall reached across the table and placed his hand

on hers.

"I wish I had that kind of faith," Ruby Ann said as she stopped herself from returning his deep gaze.

"You do. Just believe in yourself. He does, and I do, too."

Ruby Ann smiled.

Jacob sat in front of Brian's Gym and watched a beautiful blonde girl in tights walk out, climb in her car, and drive away. He got out and entered the gym and walked up to the counter. Behind the counter stood Susie, a very pretty buxom girl of about twenty, also in tights.

"Hi, may I help you?" Susie said.

Jacob flashed some ID as he looked around to see two very large men in sweat suits looking their direction as one exercised on a stepper and another on a rower.

"Hello, I'm Marley with investigations. I'm following up on some leads in a murder investigation," Jacob said.

"Murder? Whose?" Susie asked.

"I'm not at liberty to say; but it's just routine. We are checking someone's whereabouts," Jacob said.

"Oh. Whose?"

"Do you know a Lucy Mills?"

"Miss Mills? You just missed her. She's in nearly every day."

"Was she in on the sixth around two o'clock?" Jacob asked.

"Let me see," Susie said as she looked through some files. "Yes, she signed the register. Wait a minute. Hers said two, but the two before her say three o'clock … "

"So, it's possible she wasn't here at two," Jacob said.

"It is possible, but even if she was, she could have left without us knowing," Susie said.

"Could I have a copy of this?" Jacob asked.

"Sure, I'll be right back," Susie said.

Susie went to make a copy. As two muscular women in shorts and T-shirts walked by Jacob, he turned and leaned against the counter and watched them on their way. He noticed the two large men on the machines did the same, and he quickly reined his attention back, somewhat repelled to find himself aligned with them.

"Here you go," Susie said.

"Thank you, Miss. You've been a lot of help," Jacob said.

Jacob began to walk away as two more women with ripped abs crossed his path.

"Have you considered joining a club?" Susie asked.

Without turning around, Jacob shot a reply over his shoulder.

"I am now."

He walked out.

Tommy walked into to a dingy room at the Dixie Breeze.

The room was barely furnished. Shelby Lee was lying on the bed.

"We're back in business. Superior wants you back," Tommy said.

"What are you talking about?" Shelby asked.

"It's in the paper, see..." Tommy said.

She took the paper, jumped in the air, screamed, and kissed Tommy.

"They want me, they really want me!" Shelby said. They embraced.

Randall and Ruby Ann walked out of the restaurant as Jacob walked up.

"I think I found something," Jacob said.

"Oh?" Ruby Ann said.

"It looks like Lucy Mills has a pretty flimsy alibi for Wilson's murder," Jacob said.

"So, what can we do?" Ruby Ann asked.

"We've got to get the detective to look at her closer," Randall said.

"Yeah, but he won't listen to me. Ms. Wilkes, can you?" Jacob asked.

"Of course," she said, looking at her watch. "Give me what you have. I'll try to catch him today."

Joe walked up.

"Great news, they took the bait. 10 a.m.," Joe said.

"Let's hope it's in time," Randall said.

Inside Clayton's office at Superior Records, Clayton stood and spoke with Randall and Ruby Ann as Joe and Jacob stepped into the adjacent conference room.

"Are you ready?" Randall asked.

"No problem," Clayton replied.

"We'll just be inside the door," Ruby Ann said.

The intercom came on, and his assistant's voice was heard.

"Shelby Lee is here, Mr. Willows," the assistant said.

He pressed the intercom.

"Give me a moment and send her in," Clayton said.

He pressed the intercom, so it stayed on and was

heard in the conference room. Randall and Ruby Ann joined Joe and Jacob standing around the intercom receiver on a conference table in the other room.

"Loud and clear," Jacob said.

Shelby and Tommy entered Clayton's office.

"Shelby, Tommy, come in! Sit down, sit down. I'm glad to see you saw our press release," Clayton said.

The group, now seated around the conference table, listened in.

"I'm so excited about this new deal, Clayton. What have you got in mind?" Shelby asked.

"Just wait a minute. We have a few things that we need before Shelby begins," Tommy said.

"I didn't realize that you would be part of this deal, Tommy," Clayton said.

"What do you mean?" Tommy asked.

"Well, one of the things that made me interested in having Shelby come back to the label was knowing that you would not be managing her from behind bars," Clayton said.

"What do you mean?" Shelby asked.

"What's going on?" Tommy said.

"Once they convict you for Grayson's murder..." Clayton said.

"Murder?" Shelby turned to Tommy. "Why you ..."

Shelby began hitting Tommy.

"I don't know what he's talking about," Tommy said.

Randall stepped from the conference room into the office.

"You and Shelby were so broke you could barely buy groceries," Randall said. "So you decided to get even with the man who took everything from you. When you tried to steal the artifacts from Grayson's office, Tommy, he surprised you, and you killed him."

At those words, Tommy rushed from the room into the reception area, and Randall pursued him.

Randall tackled him as the assistant called for the police. The two began to fight. Randall was knocked down.

Chapter Twenty Eight

Randall rose from the floor of the Superior Records reception area and threw another punch. They exchanged a few more blows, and Tommy went down and stayed down as O'Shields entered with some other police officers. Randall looked up at him.

"This one's alive, Detective," Randall quipped.

The police carried Tommy out of the building. Clayton stood next to Shelby and Randall as Ruby Ann, Jacob, and Joe joined the group.

"Now I got the best girl singer in town. All I need is you, Randall," Clayton said.

"I don't know," Randall said.

Detective O'Shields walked up to the group.

"Sergeant Randall, I just wanted to let you know this clears up the first little charge, and with the info Ms. Wilkes gave me yesterday, we were able to persuade Wilson's girlfriend to make a plea. So, I guess you are in the clear, for now," he said.

O'Shields began to walk off but turned back to face Randall.

"One more thing. Would you mind signing this for my grandson, Patrick?"

O'Shields handed him a 45 rpm record.

"I thought that was your first name, Detective," Ruby Ann said.

Randall signed it as Ruby Ann began smiling.

"It is. It is ..." O'Shields said as he walked away.

"Thanks, Detective," Randall said.

"OK, buddyroe, you're in the clear now," Joe said. "We owe Clayton an answer."

"Before you do, come with me," Clayton said.

A Badge or an Old Guitar

Clayton led the group around the building where a beautiful new black and red Prevost tour bus was parked. He pulled a key from his pocket and unlocked the door.

"This is your new bus, Randall," Clayton said.

"Mine?" Randall asked.

"If you want it. There's plenty of room for your band," Clayton said.

"I don't have a band," Randall said.

Clayton opened the door and out stepped five musicians, all dressed alike and carrying instruments.

"Now you do," Clayton said.

Joe stepped inside to look around.

"I don't know. I'm not… " Randall said.

"If you don't take it, I will," Shelby said.

"Sounds like a sweet deal," Ruby Ann said.

"I just want to go back home, to the station, help people. Besides, being on the road, I'd miss all my friends here," Randall said.

Joe came out carrying a two-piece suit with exquisite Western embroidery.

"Look what was in the closet," Joe said.

"That's sharp," Randall said.

"You have a full wardrobe on board. I tell you what, you want to keep your little team together. Joe's already going as your tour manager … Jacob, how would you feel about heading up security?" Clayton said.

"I'd get to travel?" Jacob asked.

"To every state in the union," Clayton said.

"Great. Great, I'll do it," Jacob said.

Clayton then turned his focus on Ruby Ann.

"Ms. Wilkes … Ms. Wilkes … Let's see … Can you

196

sing background or play an instrument?"

"No, I'm afraid not. But I have been considering a career in entertainment law," Ruby Ann said.

"Great, maybe you could look over these contracts," Clayton said.

He pulled contracts from his coat pocket and handed them to Ruby Ann.

"Now, Randall, everyone's on board but you. You'll start this Saturday night at the Opry, then you're on the road for sixty days. I'm adding you to the concert tour featuring a package of Superior's top artists beginning in Louisville, Little Rock, Des Moines, Vegas, and beyond..." Clayton said.

"The Opry?" Randall echoed.

"So, what do you think, Randall?" Joe asked.

Randall looked at his companions and smiled.

"Let me have a few minutes to talk with the chief," he said.

He walked inside the bus, picked up a mobile phone, and dialed the McKinney Police Station. Chief Wilkes listened as Randall described Clayton's offer.

"I still don't know," Randall said. "What do you think? Is this part of God's plan?"

"Son, God doesn't care whether you're a policeman or a singer or a dogcatcher," the chief said. "He cares whether you love Him and whether you love those around you. The question for you is, 'How do you want to spread that love?' You are a doggone good cop. I taught you myself, and ain't nobody worn a McKinney badge since I been here that has a better nose on him than you. You can sniff out the issues, solve problems.

A Badge or an Old Guitar

"But son, this is only McKinney, population five hundred and two. 'Is there more to life than this?' Maybe not ... But maybe so. You have the chance to go out into the world and spread your wings. You helped this town your whole life. Now's your chance to help them over in the next town ... and the next and the next, and the next after that.

"The world needs people like you — singers who can make a name for themselves and still remember to tithe every Sunday, big shots who know how small they really are, who aren't afraid to look at all the shiny things they have and still give glory to the One who controls it all. The world needs people who would rather fund tutors for the Boys Club than buy another fancy sports car. It needs people who know the value of family — because they've lost their own.

"What does God want you to do? Son, you've lost everyone you had in the world and still found a path to serve Him. Right now, go find you a quiet spot, get down on your knees, and ask God to use you as he sees best." Randall nodded, and a burden seemed to lift from his shoulders.

"And son?" the chief added.

"Yes, chief?"

"Whichever path you choose, never forget that you are so much more than your station in life. It was the story of the widow woman and her two mites that Jesus prophesied would be told wherever the gospel was preached. This life isn't about what we have. It's about what we do with what we're given."

An hour later, Randall emerged from the bus and

turned to face the group who had been waiting on him. They were entertained by the musicians who gathered under a shade tree to jam. When Randall stepped off the bus, they promptly ended "I'm Walking the Floor Over You." All eyes were on him, awaiting, as each of them almost held their breath.

"Yes," he said. "Yes, let's do it."

Randall Franks

Chapter
Twenty Nine

Night had fallen on Music City, but the lights around the Opry House gave the evening a miraculous glow. Randall, Ruby Ann, Jacob, and the chief were standing in a dressing room. The five band members moved their instruments toward backstage.

"Chief, I sure am glad you could come," Randall said.

"I wouldn't miss your debut. Anyway, I hear Jim and Jesse McReynolds are on the show tonight," the chief said.

"Everything is ready for the trip, boss. There's just one thing that's been bothering me out of all this," Jacob said.

"What, Spirits?" Randall asked.

"Who bailed you out and shot at us?" Jacob asked.

"I think I can answer that," the chief said.

"Who, Uncle?" Ruby Ann asked.

"First, Ruby here is a dollar. You are now my attorney," the chief said. "I did."

"You shot at us?" Ruby Ann exclaimed.

"Not really. I arranged for bail. I watched you all leave the court building. I had a little sound effect show set up for your entertainment," the chief said.

"That explains why the police never found any bullets or casings," Jacob said.

"There were none. I knew a little noise would go a long way to get the investigation moving," the chief said.

"So what's the dollar for?" Ruby Ann asked.

"Those disturbing the peace charges can sometimes be tedious," the chief said. "Just in case."

— Joe stuck his head in from the bustling hallway.

"Three minutes! Three minutes!" Joe said.

"Ruby, have you given any thought to what I asked

you?" Randall said with a hopeful look in his eyes.

"Not now, James," Ruby Ann replied.

"James?" the chief questioned. "I haven't heard you called that since your mom ... "

The chief stopped as he realized the importance of what he said.

"Will you go with us?" Randall asked her. "Take off a couple of months."

Ruby Ann looked at her uncle, who shrugged it back to her.

"OK ..." she said.

"Great," Randall said. He shot her a wink and a smile.

Randall started toward the hallway to backstage and the chief stopped him.

"Don't forget, no matter where you go, you can still make a difference. If you need it, you've always got a home in McKinney," he said.

"Thanks, Chief."

Randall disappeared into the darkness of the wings of the Opry House stage.

"Ladies and gentlemen, making his debut appearance on the Opry singing his upcoming single on Superior, please welcome Randall!" the Bluegrass Music Hall of Fame member Jesse McReynolds said.

Randall performed his new single in an outfit glittering in the lights. His band dressed alike was behind him playing fiddle, guitar, steel guitar, mandolin, and acoustic bass.

While he sang his new song, "A Helping Hand," the audience roared. Ruby Ann and the chief watched from backstage, as did Joe and Jacob.

As Randall sang the last note, a wave of applause washed into the weariest corners of his soul, nearly knocking him off balance. A tear slipped down his cheek as he saw the path before him illuminated as never before. Nearly two thousand faces smiled back at him.

"I am sure Randall will be back to visit us again on the Opry," Jim McReynolds said, his amplified voice rising above the roar. "Ladies and gentlemen — Randall!"

"Take a bow, Randall," Jesse added.

Randall, who had already started walking off stage, caught a glimpse of the chief, Ruby Ann, Uncle Joe, and Spirits smiling and applauding in the wings. Time, it seemed, stood still for moment as he turned back to the audience once more, took off his hat, slightly bowed, and waved. Then the hands of time began turning once more as he stepped into the darkness of the wings and the sounds of Jim and Jesse's "Paradise" flowed from the stage behind him. Now, the light that was always within him shone even brighter. He would share that light no matter where his path led.

Randall Franks

Epilogue

Randall Franks — Epilogue

Randall's smiling face shone on a T-Shirt worn by Joe who was driving the bus down the road. Jacob, Ruby Ann, and Randall sat close to the front and looked out the windshield. Randall had a guitar in hand and was stringing together words for another song when he detoured onto a familiar group of words.

Joe's phone rang and he hit the button to find Clayton on the other end. They chatted as Randall's singing drew the rest of the group's attention.

"On the road again ..." Randall sang.

"I think that one's been taken already," Ruby Ann said.

"Yeah, but now we can sing it and really mean it," Joe said as he belted out the next line.

"Where are we going anyway?" Spirits asked.

"That-a-way. Just that-a-way," Randall said. "I am sure the Lord has something in store we couldn't even imagine. Who knows? There might be someone out there that needs our help."

Joe hung up and jumped into the conversation.

"Let's hope he imagines us around this traffic jam or we are going to miss the benefit show for the orphan's camp in Louisville that Clayton just called and added to our schedule," Joe said.

"See, what did I tell you?" Randall said. "On the road again ..."

The crew began to join in.

1 PETER 4:10

As every man hath received the gift, even so minister the same one to another, as good stewards of the manifold grace of God.

MARK 16:15

And he said unto them, Go ye into all the world, and preach the gospel to every creature.

Is There More to Life Than This

Verse One

Looking out the window you see things that can turn your heart to stone
In the pouring rain a little girl cries for her mama, who left her all alone
A brother kills a brother. For what reason, we may never know
Two who loved each other, burn themselves out of house and home

Chorus

Is there more than life than this?
I tell you my friend there is, he gave his only son and then
A chance for us to live again
A heart that is like new, that sees the good in all we do
Yes my friend, there is so much more than this

Verse Two

Two men stand upon a stage calling one another names
Each of them is asking for my vote
What happened to the kind of man who wrote the words that built this land
And filled the hearts of everyone with hope
A woman sells her soul for drugs to find a place where she is loved
At least that's what she thinks
If she awakes tomorrow, she will still see all the sorrow
That was there before she went to sleep

Is There More to Life Than This

Verse Three

Children who pick up a gun to get even with everyone
who filled their little lives with hurt
Men and women do the same because things don't go
their way
Getting back at the folks at work
Someone with wealth and fame finds no comfort in his
name
And looks for ways to change the way he feels
Deep in the darkness, he leaves us far behind and
We wonder what was on his mind

Bridge

Like the smell of the flowers
The touch of mama's hand
A fishing trip with daddy
Sunday morning hymns
A love that lasts forever
Like Grandma and Grandpa's did
The smile of a baby
Yes my friend there is much more than this
So much more than this

About the Author

Actor/entertainer Randall Franks is best known as "Officer Randy Goode" from TV's "In the Heat of the Night," a role he performed on NBC and CBS from 1988–1993. He also starred in two other series, the most recent with Robert Townsend in "Musical Theater of Hope" which aired on UPtv (Gospel Music Channel).

© 2011 Randall Franks Media — Teryl Jackson

He has co-starred or starred in 15 films with superstars who include Dolly Parton, Christian Slater, William Hurt, Stella Parton, and legendary western star "Doc" Tommy Scott. His most recent film is "Broken" with Soren Fulton, Felix Ryan, Bailey Anne Borders and Joe Stevens.

Franks' musical stylings have been heard in 150 countries and by more than 25 million Americans. The Independent Country Music Hall of Fame member's musical career boasts 25 album releases, 21 singles, and over 200 recordings with artists from various genres. The International Bluegrass Music Museum Legend annually hosts the historic Grand Master Fiddler Championship at the Country Music Hall of Fame and Museum in Nashville, Tennessee. The award-winning fiddler's best-selling release, "Handshakes and Smiles," was a top 20 Christian music seller. Many of his albums were among the top 30 bluegrass recordings of their release year. The Atlanta Country Music Hall of Fame member shared a top country vocal collaboration with Grand Ole Opry stars The Whites. In addition to his solo career, which includes years of guest starring for the Grand Ole Opry, Franks is a former member of Bill Monroe's Blue Grass Boys and Jim and Jesse's Virginia Boys. He has performed with Jeff & Sheri Easter, the Lewis Family, the Marksmen Quartet, the Watkins Family, Elaine and Shorty, "Doc" Tommy Scott's Last Real Old Time Medicine Show, and Doodle and the Golden River Grass.

He is past chairman of the Catoosa Citizens for Literacy, which assists individuals in learning to read and pursuing a GED at its Catoosa County Learning Center near Ringgold. He is also president of the Share America Foundation, Inc. that provides the Pearl and Floyd Franks Scholarship to musicians continuing the traditional music of Appalachia. He hosts a concert series at the historic Ringgold Depot which helps fund the scholarships. He is the Northwest Georgia Joint Economic Development Authority film industry liaison. He also serves on the Georgia Production Partnership Government Relations Committee.

He authored eight other books, including "Encouragers I: Finding the Light," "Encouragers II: Walking with the Masters," "Encouragers III: A Guiding Hand," "A Mountain Pearl: Appalachian Reminiscing and Recipes;" "Whittlin' and Fiddlin' My Own Way: The Violet Hensley Story" with Violet Hensley; "Stirring Up Success with a Southern Flavor," and "Stirring Up Additional Success with a Southern Flavor" with Shirley Smith; and "Snake Oil, Superstars and Me" with "Doc"

About the Author

Tommy Scott and Shirley Noe Swiesz.

A journalist with more than 20 state and national awards, Franks is also a syndicated columnist with his "Southern Style" appearing weekly in newspapers from North Carolina to Texas and at www.randallfranks.com. He was included among his generation's leading country humorists in the Loyal Jones book "Country Music Humorists and Comedians."

For more information, visit www.randallfranks.com and www.shareamericafoundation.org.

Be sure to visit Randall Franks on the web:

Randall Franks on Twitter
https://twitter.com/RandallFranks
Randall Franks Fan Page on Facebook
www.facebook.com/pages/Randall-Franks/41082829233
Randall Franks on YouTube:
http://www.youtube.com/user/randallfranks
Randall Franks at IMDB:
http://www.imdb.com/name/nm0291684/

Randall Franks as "Officer Randy Goode"
from TV's "In the Heat of the Night"

217

Order more at RandallFranks.com

"A Mountain Pearl: Appalachian
Reminiscing and Recipes"

<u>Encouragers Series</u>
<u>with Celebrity Stories, Photos and Recipes</u>

"Encouragers I: Finding the Light"
"Encouragers II: Walking with the Masters"
"Encouragers III: A Guiding Hand"

<u>Co-author of Autobiographies</u>

"Whittlin' and Fiddlin' My Own Way:
The Violet Hensley Story"

"Snake Oil, Superstars and Me"
The Story of Ramblin' "Doc" Tommy Scott
with "Doc" Tommy Scott and Shirley Noe Swiesz